FANTASTIC FOOTBALL PHENOMENA

A Red Fox Book

Published by Random House Children's Books
20 Vauxhall Bridge Road, London SW1V 2SA

A division of Random House UK Ltd
London Melbourne Sydney Auckland
Johannesburg and agencies throughout the world

First published in Great Britain by Red Fox 1998

Printed and bound in Great Britain by Cox & Wyman Ltd, Reading, Berkshire

Papers used by Random House UK Limited are natural, recyclable products made from wood grown in sustainable forests. The manufacturing processes conform to the environmental regulations of the country of origin.

RANDOM HOUSE UK Limited Reg. No. 954009

ISBN 0 09 926432 3

FANTASTIC FOOTBALL PHENOMENA

Tim Barnett

Illustrated by Phil Healey

CONTENTS

ACKNOWLEDGEMENTS

The Author would like to thank the following people, without whom this project would never have got off the ground.

First and foremost, my editor at Red Fox, Kate Tym, whose patient promptings ensured that everything happened more or less when it was supposed to. Also, special thanks to Bernard Bale whose input is greatly appreciated. Others include: Marie Arymar – for her encouragement and proof-reading – Steve Pearce, Ian Piercy and all at *Final Score*: you couldn't ask for better back-up. To Peter Taylor, Vince Hilaire and Ian Wright for making the Palace palatable for all those years and, finally, to the late Reg Hayter for making it all possible in the first place. Thanks one and all.

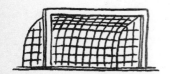

INTRODUCTION

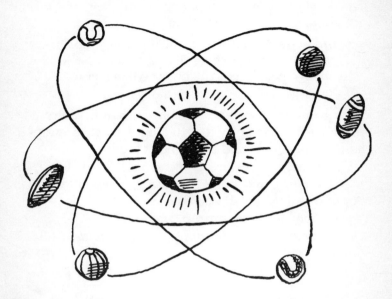

Let's get one thing straight before we start – football *is fantastic*. You already know that, or else you wouldn't have picked up this book. But, believe it or not, there are people out there who simply don't realise quite how *fantastic* football can be.

It is, quite simply, the most phenomenal game in the world. Other sports are just fantastically dull in comparison ...

- ⊕ *rugby* – too many players, funny-shaped balls that don't bounce properly and silly songs. Make it eleven-a-side, give them a round ball and get the fans to learn some decent ditties.

- ⊕ *cricket* – boring! They need numbers and names on the back of their shirts and a bit of physical contact to make it more exciting. Make the ball bigger (and softer) and have goals instead of wickets.

⚽ *basketball* – you've got to be at least 100 feet tall to be a basketball player! It would be much better if you could only use your feet to play the ball. And those nets are just too high. How about turning them on their side, making them bigger and putting them on the ground?

⚽ *tennis* – you've got to be called Tarquin Cholmondley-Westington, or something like it, to join the local club. Keep the nets – get rid of everything else (including Tarquin).

Other games *can* be fun occasionally (like if you've got a broken leg and can't play football), but football is always the winner in my book, and in this book too.

Within these pages are tremendous tales of footballing fun, facts, fights, frolics and foul-ups. And the most amazing thing is that they are all true!

Read them, tell them to your family and friends and enjoy them. But most of all, enjoy football – it is *fantastic*, after all!

Although today football is the world's most *fantastic* game, there is some argument about when and where it originated.

The British often claim to have 'invented' football, but all they really did was gather together lots of existing games, put them into a big pot and cook up an organised sport from all the different ingredients.

Once they had done that, the British exported their new game around the world – and everybody started beating them at it.

Of course, being a nation of such good sports, they quickly decided to invent other games – like cricket and rugby – and let the rest of the world beat them at those too.

But it was football that caught the imagination of everybody from Torquay to Timbuktu (except the Americans of course. They went off and invented 'world championships' in games that only they play).

What is certain is that civilisations as long ago as the ancient Chinese, Greeks and Romans played games that involved some sort of ball skills: although anybody watching them wouldn't recognise them as what we call 'football' today.

There is a story that the ancient Chinese, when they were playing away from home, would cut off the heads of beaten opponents and kick them around the battleground — it gave a whole new meaning to players

losing their heads during a match. They often lost their fingers, arms and legs, too.

Although it made for good sport (unless you were the player left with an empty neck), it's unlikely that even the most lenient refs would let players get away with tactics like that today.

Elsewhere in the Far East there were dozens of pastimes where players had to juggle the ball with feet, legs and head and direct it through big metal rings or holes in walls or curtains.

In England, though, there was no place for such delicacies as skill or technique. You took your life in your hands if you took part in the early ball games, which were often between entire villages – that's a couple of hundred-a-side ... and no ref to save you when things went wrong.

The reason there was no ref was simple – there were no rules.

For someone to blow a whistle and mutter 'I say, chaps, that was jolly unfair. Please don't do it again,' would have been about as much use as asking the Roman army to stop and take their shoes off before coming in and wrecking your house.

Fortunately for the police, stewards and crowd control experts of the day, matches only took place about once a year – probably because it took everyone that long to recover between games! Just imagine if they played twice a week like they do now!

PHENOMENAL PHACT!

In England in the Middle Ages a public brawl could result in a death sentence for the person held responsible for starting it. So it's no surprise that people were so keen to take part in a sport where violence was all part and parcel of the game: it was great at getting rid of tension. Times have changed though, and these days some players get rewarded with huge pay cheques for starting brawls every week.

Blimey! and I thought boxing was dangerous

1 FANTASTIC FOOTBALL CLUBS

Of course, most football fans follow one club or another – and much as we like to admire pin-point passing, dynamic defenders and glorious goals, the odds are that we more often see slow stoppers, puzzled playmakers and sloppy strikers.

But the thing is ... we don't care! So long as our team wins, we're generally not that bothered how they do it. Of course, the better the football, the better the buzz. But 'It's not the winning it's the taking part that counts?' Forget it.

Most fans would be as happy seeing their team beat the League leaders with a last second deflection off the striker's bottom as with a beautifully crafted 25-yard screamer. And that's the beauty of the game – you never know what's coming next. It's *phenomenal*!

Ever since time began clubs have been breaking records and setting targets ...

When **Blackpool** came back from 3-1 down with 20 minutes to go against **Bolton** to win the FA Cup in 1953, it was thanks in no small part to the brilliant wing play of the legendary Stanley Matthews. Due to Matthews' extravagant skills in setting up that historic win the game became known as the 'Matthews Final' - despite the fact that forward Stan Mortensen scored a hat-trick for the Seasiders. Many felt that Mortensen was hard done by to miss out on the glory, and upon his death in 1991 the *Guardian* newspaper commented that his memorial service was likely to be dubbed 'The Matthews Funeral'.

Whisper it quietly, but **Everton** played a huge role in the creation of their great rivals **Liverpool**. Having won their first League Championship in 1891 whilst playing at their second stadium, Anfield, Everton had a major bust-up with landlord John Houlding who wanted to increase their rent from £100 per year to a mammoth £250 per year! They promptly upped and left, moving to a field called Mere Green to the north of the city's Stanley Park. But John Houlding was not to be that easily beaten and he quickly started a new club at Anfield – and even tried to call them Everton. The FA wouldn't allow that, so he reluctantly switched the name to Liverpool.

And you can quote me on that ...
Legendary Liverpool boss Bill Shankly made no secret of his disregard for the Reds' neighbours, Everton. Among many insults he handed out to the men from Goodison Park he once said:
'If Everton were playing at the bottom of my garden, I'd draw the curtains.' To which he later added: 'There are two teams worth watching in this city. Liverpool and Liverpool reserves.'

It's hard to believe these days, but **Manchester United** were once one of the poorest clubs in the country, and on the verge of going broke and having to leave their Bank Street ground. Away trips could often only take place after a collection among the fans and the club was in serious danger of folding until they were rescued ... by a St. Bernard dog! More typically the saviour of stranded mountaineers, the St. Bernard was 'employed' at a fund-raising event by the club to wander round proceedings with a collection box about its neck - but the dog got lost and ended up on the doorstep of wealthy local businessman, John Davies. Mr Davies traced the dog's owner – club captain Harry Stafford – and was told all about the club's cash crisis. He promptly paid off their debts, became chairman and instigated the move to Old Trafford in 1902. Simple eh?!

ANIMAL ATTRACTION

Dogs on the pitch regularly disturb matches, even today, from park level right up to senior games. And, in the early days of football, goats, chickens, geese and even cows would occasionally stop by for a look at the action, or to munch a particularly tasty looking tuft of grass. But it was a swarm of killer bees which interrupted Zimbabwe's Africa Cup qualifier against Ghana in Harare. With impeccable taste, the buzzing arrivals ignored the players and made a 'bee-line' straight for the ref and his linesmen as the officials were leaving the field at half-time.

Talking of animals, football is so popular in Denmark that even the pigs play it! Danish pig farmers have discovered that their animals are healthier and more happy if they are given something to do ... and it seems that their favourite pastime, like mine and yours, is knocking a ball about. There is even a company which now makes hard-wearing footballs just for pigs! Wonder if some of the porkers will one day play for West *Ham,* or *Swine*-Don Town, or would The *Trotters* of Bolton be more their style?

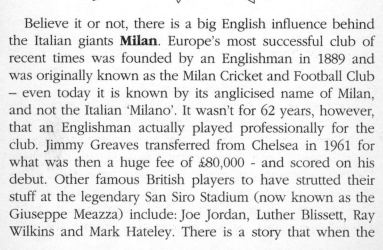

Believe it or not, there is a big English influence behind the Italian giants **Milan**. Europe's most successful club of recent times was founded by an Englishman in 1889 and was originally known as the Milan Cricket and Football Club – even today it is known by its anglicised name of Milan, and not the Italian 'Milano'. It wasn't for 62 years, however, that an Englishman actually played professionally for the club. Jimmy Greaves transferred from Chelsea in 1961 for what was then a huge fee of £80,000 - and scored on his debut. Other famous British players to have strutted their stuff at the legendary San Siro Stadium (now known as the Giuseppe Meazza) include: Joe Jordan, Luther Blissett, Ray Wilkins and Mark Hateley. There is a story that when the

club signed **Watford** star Luther Blissett they actually meant to capture his team-mate, the former England winger John Barnes – but got the wrong player!

Comfortably the biggest football club in the world, the supporters and followers of **Barcelona** could be forgiven for believing that their team really does occasionally benefit from some 'divine intervention'. Boasting a whopping 110,000 club members, and even its own bank, Barcas – as the club is known – is effectively the national side for the Catalan region. Their immense Nou Camp stadium holds 115,000 spectators, second in size only to the awesome

Estadio da Luz (Stadium of Light) of **Benfica** in neighbouring Portugal. This is all well and good – but God on their side? Well, the belief stems from the fact that 'God's representative on earth' Pope John Paul II, was recently enrolled as club member number 108,000! Barcelona's argument may not hold sway in several other places however – at their various clubs the following players have all been known simply as 'God': Franco Baresi (Milan), Robbie Fowler (Liverpool) and, perhaps most incredibly of all, Mick Harford (Luton Town).

In the early part of the 20th century, **Newcastle** were a particularly superstitious bunch. They believed that if they saw a wedding on the way to a match then they were sure to win, while a funeral signalled a defeat. There were those that suggested that if United could just avoid churches on their pre-match journey then they would draw every week.

QUESTION

In the 1994/95 season Newcastle led the Premiership by 12 points in January but still failed to win the title. True or False?

While lots of old people go on about how great the 1960s were, you won't find too many **Northampton** fans to agree with them. The Cobblers experienced an extraordinary decade which saw them promoted from Division Four in 1961, going on to reach the First Division by 1965. However, their fall from grace was just as quick and by 1969 Northampton were back where they'd started – in the bottom division once more.

Luton Town certainly had the 'rub of the green' when they played their first ever game at their current Kenilworth Road ground. The Hatters played Plymouth – who wore green – the referee was a Mr Green, the game was kicked-off by a local brewer called Green and the club secretary at the time was called … yep, you've guessed it!

Oxford United took part in the longest FA Cup-Tie on record in 1970/71. Their Fourth Round Qualifying tie against Alvechurch took 6 matches and 11 hours to complete, and as if they weren't knackered enough after that marathon, Oxford eventually lost 1–0.

One of the world's most famous clubs, **Preston North End** were founder members of the Football League and won the League and FA Cup 'double' in the competition's first year. Two years previously, in 1887, they had demolished Hyde 26–0 in the FA Cup – a record score for a competitive match in England. Legend has it that the referee lost his watch during the game, and as a result that match lasted 15 minutes longer than it should have. It's an excuse for Hyde, but not much of one, and just imagine what Alex Ferguson, with his famous stopwatch, would have made of it!

Scottish giants **Rangers** are without doubt their country's leading side of the past decade. By the end of the 1996/97 campaign they had won an equal record (with **Celtic**) nine League titles in a row as well as a host of other trophies and their large and increasing bank balance would seem to guarantee them further glory. However, we need to hark back to 1898/99 to recall the 'Gers most successful ever season. That year they won all 18 of their League fixtures – a feat considered to be a world record.

Caledonian Thistle are the youngest League club in Britain, having formed in 1994 to join the Scottish Third Division. The club is made up of two former sides, Inverness Caledonian and Inverness Thistle, and the Inverness club made a small piece of history of their own way back in 1895 when they took part in the shortest Scottish game of all time. Thistle scored a controversial goal just two minutes into a League match against Citadel, and the Citadel players were so angry they walked off the field in disgust!

Cardiff City have the distinction of being the only club from outside England ever to have won the FA Cup – but although they hailed from Wales, the Bluebirds had only three Welshmen in their side when they beat Arsenal 1-0 in the 1927 competition. Their side was also made up of four Irishmen, three Scots and an Englishman. Three years earlier the club had almost completed an ever greater feat, when they finished runners-up in the League to **Huddersfield Town** on goal average. Talk about needing calculators – Cardiff lost out by just 0.024 of a goal! Now that's close.

What's in a name?

Sheffield Wednesday are the only football club to have named themselves after a day of the week - and it wasn't even Saturday! The club was formed by members of the Sheffield Wednesday Cricket Club, who only met on Wednesday half-holidays.

But if you think that Wednesday is a weird name for a football club, take a look at some of these...

- ⚽ **In Albania there is a club called 17 Nentori Tirana, which means 17th November. The club was named after the date of the country's Independence Day.**

- ⚽ **One of Switzerland's most successful sides is a team called Young Boys.**

- ⚽ **The Colo-Colo club of Chile is not, as many people think, sponsored by a local fizzy drink manufacturer. It is actually named after the local nickname for a wildcat.**

- ⚽ **Ghanaian club Hearts of Oak got their unusual title from the British gold mining pioneers of 1891 who founded the side.**

- ⚽ **The Strongest is the hopeful name of one of Bolivia's leading sides, who were founded in 1908 and hold the record number of Bolivian title wins.**

Sadly, 19 of the club's players perished in an air crash in the Andes mountains in 1969.

⚽ The Dutch League boasts a club called Go Ahead Eagles, which has won the national championship on four occasions.

⚽ Grasshoppers is hardly a name to strike fear into the hearts of opponents, but this Swiss club are one of Europe's finest.

⚽ The Mighty Blackpool is the name of a club in Sierra Leone, which was formed by supporters of the club who hail from the English seaside town of Blackpool.

⚽ Nicknames are often good for a laugh. The Jam Tarts of Hearts takes some beating, but what about Germany's FC Koln? How would you like to play for a side called 'The Billygoats'. Suppose it would be alright for Nicky Butt.

⚽ And talking of nicknames, Czechoslovakian club Bohemians are to this day known as 'The Kangaroos', even though the marsupial has never been seen outside captivity in Eastern Europe. The club acquired the name following an early tour of Australia, during which the players were presented with the gift of two live kangaroos as a souvenir of their visit.

During the reign of Italian dictator Mussolini, **Inter Milan** were forced to change their name. They used to be called Internazionale until quite recently, but while Mussolini was around they were called Ambrosiana after St Ambrogio, the patron saint of Milan. Mussolini believed that the name 'Internazionale' reflected Marxist-thinking.

QUESTION

In which country would you be if you were watching a club called O'Higgins play a home game?

Good Sports

Many clubs were first formed by enthusiasts of other sports, who simply wanted another hobby to kill time when they couldn't take part in their first choice pastime. Here's a look at some clubs which exist 'by accident'.

⚽ The world's first club, Sheffield FC, only came about because members of the Sheffield Cricket Club wanted something to do during the winter months.

⚽ Slavia Prague began life as a gymnastics and cycling club at the end of the 19th century, but between 1905 and 1938 they won the Czech title nine times under the same manager. His name was Harry Madden, a Scotsman.

⚽ Brazilian outfits Flamengo and Vasco Da Gama both had the same beginnings – they were started by members of yachting clubs who wanted something to do on land.

⚽ Galatasaray are not just one of Turkey's biggest soccer clubs, they also own an island where their rowing club is based, and a water complex which is home to their swimming and water polo teams. In fact, the club has a section for just about any major sport you care to think of.

Answer: Chile! The club is named after a Chilean revolutionary who is a national hero and went on to lead the country in the early 19th century. He is of Irish descent and our equivalent would be if Nottingham Forest were renamed Robin Hood.

QUESTION

Sport and religion have strong links, too, with many clubs being formed by churches to give young men of the day a sporting aim. Which of these clubs do you think began life as church teams?

Aston Villa   Barnsley   Bolton Wanderers
Brighton   Everton   Fulham   Millwall

Answer: All of them except Brighton, which was formed in a pub, and Millwall, which came about thanks to the workers of a local marmalade factory!

FANTASTIC FOOTBALL FIGHTBACKS

There is nothing more satisfying in football than coming back when all seemed lost and winning the game. Not only does it put points on the board, but it also gives you ample opportunity to taunt the supporters of the opposition ...

In the South American Club Cup of 1983, Argentinian side Estudiantes had two men sent off in the first-half of their tie against Gremio of Brazil. With 20 minutes to go, Gremio were 3-1 ahead. Estudiantes had two more players sent off, but fought back to tie the game 3-3 – with just seven players left on the field!

But few football fightbacks can match the one achieved by Charlton Athletic on 21st December 1957. With 28 minutes left on the clock, Charlton were 5-1 down at home to Huddersfield Town in a Division Two match, having been reduced to ten men since the 15th minute. Incredibly, Charlton went from that seemingly impossible situation to winning the match 7-6, inspired by winger Johnny Summers who scored five goals! Huddersfield remain the only team to score six times in a League match and lose.

Other extraordinary turnarounds include QPR drawing 5-5 at home to Newcastle on 22nd September 1984 after being 4-0 down at half-time, and Ipswich Town earning a point at Barnsley in March 1996 having been 3-0 down with just five minutes left.

Fans of Greek giants **Panathinaikos** are used to success. So much so that they held a mass demonstration after their side lost a League game 0-1 to Kalamata. They were not protesting about the defeat itself but the fact that their side had 'slumped' to second place in the table!

Italian club **Perugia** are not a side who have enjoyed limitless success since their inception in 1905. But they seemed to be on the brink of the big time in season 1978/79, when they enjoyed a phenomenal season, going the entire League game of 30 games unbeaten. But even a run like that couldn't win them the Serie A title, and they finished runners-up to AC Milan, who were three points ahead despite losing three times.

Paying the Penalty?

Before 1891 the shout of 'It's got to be a penalty ref!' was routinely ignored by referees the world over. There was a good reason for this – the spot-kick hadn't been invented. Before then, it was within the rules to stop a player in the penalty area just about any way you could think of. Even after the penalty had been introduced it didn't always benefit the victims. If the award was made late in a game an opposing player would often simply boot the ball out of the ground, leaving the ref's watch to tick away and the final whistle to blow!

But since then, penalties have become a major part of the world game, deciding many vital matches...

⚽ The world record for the number of legitimate penalties awarded in a single game is six. All the kicks came in a Cypriot First Division match between Omonia Nicosia and Olympiakos, when the teams 'won' three decisions each. All the spot-kicks were scored and the game finished 6-4 to Omonia.

⚽ A scientific study of World Cups 1982, 1986, 1990 and 1994 showed that a goalkeeper has only a 14 per cent chance of saving a penalty-kick.

⚽ The first major tournament decided on penalties was the 1976 European Championship, when Czechoslovakia beat West Germany 5-3 in the shoot-out. Ice cool Czech player Panenka netted the historic winner – with a chip into the middle of the net!

⚽ Penalty shoot-outs have produced shocks, excitement and tears many times since, but never more successful shots than in November 1988. Argentinos Juniors and Racing Club were engaged in a game which required a penalty decider and there were an incredible 44 kicks taken before a result was reached – Argentinos won 20-19.

UP
FOR
THE
CUP

A lot of people think that penalty shoot-outs are no way to decide a match – but what is the answer to settling a stalemate?

When **Bristol City** met **Cardiff City** in a Wartime Cup-Tie the powers-that-be decided that if the scores were deadlocked after 90 minutes the sides would simply play on until somebody scored a goal. Exhausted Cardiff finally won the match – courtesy of a strike after 202 minutes!

However, that's nothing compared to the longest game in the history of organised football in England, which coincidentally also took place in the Wartime Cup. When **Stockport** played **Doncaster** on 23rd March 1946 they played for a staggering 500 minutes (that's more than eight-and-a-half hours!) before finally abandoning the game with the score stuck at 2-2. Legend has it that many supporters went to do their shopping, have their hair cut or eat their tea before coming back to watch the rest of the match!

When Santos of Brazil played Uruguayan club Penarol in a South American Cup tie some years ago it was similarly agreed to play on until somebody scored. After playing for three-and-a-half hours with the scores stuck at 3-3 the teams finally gave up and a replay was decided upon.

CLUBS NEED TO EXORCISE

Often described as a 'Sleeping Giant' Birmingham City have spent much of their existence more comatose than asleep. Indeed, their lengthy kip would put Rip Van Winkle to shame. Since foundation in 1875 Blues' only major trophy has been the 1963 League Cup – but there could be a good reason. Gypsies were said to have put a curse on the club after being evicted from the site of the St. Andrews ground at the turn of the century. During the early 1980s manager Ron Saunders was so desperate for a turnaround in fortunes that he had the bottom of the players' boots painted red in a bid to ward off evil spirits.

Now firmly installed in their spanking new Pride Park Stadium, Derby County will be hoping that their new surroundings help rid them of the tag of being one of the country's unluckiest sides. The Rams – their nickname – have played in 13 FA Cup Semi-Finals, yet have reached the Final just four times, winning the famous old trophy only once. That victory came against Charlton in 1946, after captain Jack Nicholas had pleaded with local Romany gypsies to lift a curse which had been placed on the club in 1895. Derby had kicked the gypsies off the site of their old Baseball Ground stadium. However, since the lights went out halfway through their first ever match at the new ground – against Wimbledon in August 1997 – maybe there's life in the old curse yet.

And a curse is also said to hang over Priestfield Stadium, home of Gillingham. It's existence dates back to the 1940s, when a motor accident involving the club's then manager, Archie Clarke, resulted in the death of a young gypsy girl in one of the streets surrounding the ground. Almost fifty, mainly success-starved, years later the Gills appointed Kevin McElhinney - a catholic priest - to exorcise the curse ... and the club promptly won their next three home games.

The clubs have thrown up some *phenomenal* tales down the years. But none of us would get the enjoyment we do out of football without the best efforts of all the players, managers and coaches – good, bad and indifferent - who have put their all into the game over the years.

Coming next, some of the fantastic folk who have all helped, in their own little way, to put the game of football where it is today...

FANTASTIC FOOTBALL FLASHBACK

Football wasn't the only thing undergoing great upheaval during the sport's formative years. The whole world was busy finding its feet, and England – the birthplace of the modern game – was no different.

Between the short-lived reign of soccer-hater Edward II and the football-friendly arrival of Charles II on the throne, no fewer than 15 monarchs take their place as head of state over 333 years of historical happenings. On top of that there are also the cunning Cromwells - Oliver and Richard – who rule the land as 'Lord Protectors' for eleven years.

While early day midfielders and goalkeepers are fighting for their right to play the game, there are battles of a different kind raging all across the globe. The Scots will remember the Battle of Bannockburn – away victory over England – while there is also the 100 Years War, the War of the Roses, the Battle of Agincourt (England 1, France 0) and the sinking of the Spanish Armada (England 1, Spain 0) to contend with. Much later comes the Battle of Waterloo, where Wellington boots Napoleon up the backside to give England a 2-0 advantage over the French.

The Bubonic Plague (cleverly known as the Black Death, because it gives you black spots and it kills you) is the mother of all diseases, seeing around two million Britons lose their lives, and, while wanna-be strikers across the country are trying not to lose their heads in front of goal, two of the infamous Henry VIII's six wives really do … lose their heads.

Meanwhile, quietly in the background behind the ever-changing monarchs and furious fighting, a new sport which will eventually enthral the world is beginning to take shape …

Early 14th Century King Edward II was more of an archery fan, and he issued a royal decree banning the game of football. He was worried about the large number of fit young men who became seriously unfit after being trampled on playing football and were unable to report for army training. He said they should concentrate on 'more worthwhile' pursuits like archery. Some people thought he must have shares in the local bow and arrow-making company.

1583 The Puritans (a bunch of killjoys who liked you having fun even less than someone who really doesn't like you having very much fun at all) became alarmed that if so many people were playing this game, then they must be enjoying it. Couldn't have that. So the game was also banned by the church. Needless to say, that just made everyone want to play it more.

Do you get moaned at for being a football-obsessed philistine? Just listen to what 16th century Puritan Phillip Stubbes had to say: 'For as concerning footballe playing, I protest unto you it may be rather called a friendlie kinde of fyghte than a play or recreation, a bloody or murmuring practise than a fellowly sporte or pastime.'

1660 At last! A sensible king turned up. Charles II – bless him – encouraged football (and hated Puritans), after it had been banned by the previous *seven* football-phobic monarchs.

1793　Six players from Sheffield took on six players from Norton in a match which lasted *three days* and ended in huge amounts of violence and near death. It was a great match and a taste of 'derby' games today.

1815　The game of football as we know it began to emerge in public schools (which means private schools) and Universities (which means Universities). Unfortunately, all the schools played to different rules, but, hey, what the heck. At Rugby, for example, players were allowed to handle the ball but not run with it, while at Westminster there were no goals, just a line for the ball to be kicked over.

> **PHENOMENAL PHACT!**

Even today there is a game every year which goes back to the earliest days of football. Each Shrove Tuesday – better known as Pancake Day – two halves of the town of Ashbourne in Derbyshire face each other in a free-for-all. The 'goals' are the gates of Ashbourne Hall, at one end of town, and the Parish Church at the other. The aim of the game is simply to force the ball to the other team's goal by whatever means necessary.

Eton Wall Game

The pupils at Eton College, being posh and rich and so not having to take any notice of what anybody else thought, made up their own game, cunningly called the Eton Wall Game. Fancy a go? Well here's how ...

① Find a wall about 120 yards long, and mark out a pitch no wider than 6 yards.

② Make a 'goal' at each end (at Eton they use a small door and a tree).

③ Pick a team – don't worry about leaving anyone out, the whole school can play. The more the merrier. One team should line up at each end of the pitch.

④ Ask someone who's not playing – and who doesn't mind getting squashed – to drop a ball in the middle.

⑤ *Charge!*

⑥ The object is to score a goal by getting the ball to the other team's end – however you like, really. If you've got it right, you should score about every two years.

2 FANTASTIC FOOTBALL FOLK

We've seen how the game started to evolve, and a little bit about the clubs that compete around the world.

But where would the game of football be without the players themselves - those brave and hardy souls who trot out each week to live out the dreams and, perhaps more often, the nightmares of the watching crowd ...

GA-GA GOALKEEPERS

They say that you have to be mad to be a goalkeeper, and former Coventry and Hereford stopper **David Icke** certainly had a few people wondering when he claimed to be the Son of God in 1991. Icke insisted that he had been placed as God's messenger on earth, and that all his followers – which only seemed to include his wife, girlfriend and family – should dress in turquoise tracksuits and follow certain 'life rules' laid down by God, through him.

And what about the crazy Colombian **Rene Higuita**, who famously saved a Jamie Redknapp shot with his athletic 'scorpion-kick', which involved doing a handspring and hooking the ball away with his ankles? It was certainly athletic, even if the linesman's flag was already up. But, as former England goalie Gordon Banks said at the time: "What's wrong with a simple catch? If he'd done that playing

for England Jack Charlton would have punched him on the nose and he'd have never won another cap.' Famous for his unconventional methods, Higuita was also caught out at the 1990 World Cup when he tried to dribble the ball around Cameroon's Roger Milla – near the halfway line! Milla promptly robbed him and ran 40 yards with the ball before scoring the goal which knocked Colombia out of the competition.

Former Everton and Wales 'keeper **Dai Davies** gave up shot-stopping and took up alternative medicine, using his new found skills to massage people's minds and bodies and ease away their troubles. He also studied the secret life of plants to aid in treatment at his health centre, in Llangollen, North Wales. But Davies insisted: 'I couldn't be happier. People say 'keepers are barmy, and if they think I am, good luck to them. I can help with pain, either spiritual or physical. People say David Icke is off his head, but they should take time to read his books before making a judgement. I don't receive messages from God, but I do

believe there is a spirit watching over us all.' Beats opening a pub I suppose.

Mad would also perhaps be a bit unfair on well-travelled 'keeper **John Burridge** – a man who once described the sound of the ball hitting the net as 'the old death rattle' – but he could certainly be described as, well, eccentric. By the beginning of the 1997/98 campaign Burridge had played for no less than 24 professional clubs in Britain, over a 29-year career which began at Workington way back in 1968/69. But he is still as in love with the game today as he was all those years ago.

Among the many tales telling of 'Budgie's' joy in playing is the story that, in his prime, he used to go and watch every single England international at Wembley – taking his football boots with him, just in case all three 'keepers in the squad were injured before the game! And his wife once revealed that John often slept in his kit, with a football next to the bed. But the final word must go to the great man himself. 'When I came into the game as a 15-year-old, one of the trainers said to me: "Son, goalkeepers have got to be crackers and daft. You, son, have got the qualities of an international." I took it as a compliment.' Quite.

One of Chelsea's first captains was the enormous **Willie 'Fatty' Foulke**, who was 6ft 3in tall and weighed a whopping 20 stone! A giant in every sense of the word he sparked off the first official use of ball-boys. His manager at the time, John Tait Robertson, claimed that the presence of two small boys behind the goal made 'Fatty' look even bigger – but I reckon it's because the lardy 'keeper couldn't be bothered to run after the ball when it went off. At Sheffield United, Foulke once turned up early at the team hotel and ate his pre-match meal – and those of six of his team-mates!

Jose Luis Chilavert is a Paraguayan soccer star who plays for Argentinian side Velez Sarsfield. He takes all his side's penalties, and free-kicks from within shooting range, and is believed to possess the deadliest shot in the country. He has also been voted by 120 coaches as the best *Goalkeeper* in the world.

The thing with being a goalkeeper is that you spend a lot of time leaping around in muddy puddles pulling off spectacular saves, right? Wrong. Spanish international 'keeper Zamora, who played back in the 1930s, hated dirt and mess so much that he often took a broom out onto the field of play to sweep his goalmouth!

1920s 'keeper **Dan Lewis** is the man responsible for an Arsenal tradition which lives on to this very day. In the 1927 FA Cup Final against Cardiff, Gunners coach Tom Whittaker blamed Lewis's shiny new shirt for the goal which lost Arsenal the cup. Lewis seemed to have gathered the ball safely, when it slipped off his chest and into the net. From that day onward no Arsenal goalkeeper has ever taken to the field in a brand new jersey.

NEW BALLS PLEASE

A women's soccer match in Sora, Italy, erupted into violence when the home team's goalie was discovered to be ... a man! When the female 'keeper failed to turn up, the team's male coach, Piero Pucci, donned a wig, stuffed a couple of tennis balls in place and pretended to be the reserve. When the opposition became suspicious they suddenly grabbed him and made an on the spot inspection.

DODGY DEFENDERS

We all know that football is a physical game, and as such it has its risks. But Lyon defender **Jean-Luc Sassus** could be forgiven for not seeing one particular injury coming. Jean-Luc was rushed to hospital during match in January 1997 after being punched by another player ... his own goalkeeper, Pascal Oimeta.

And what about the famous bust-up in 1995, when Blackburn Rovers' England pair **David Batty** and **Graeme Le Saux** started trading punches during a European Cup match against Moscow Spartak. A disagreement between the pair caused the rift, prompting Spartak manager Oleg Romantsev to say: 'Before this match I told my players that they would be playing against 11 men ready to fight for each other for 90 minutes. I didn't expect them to be fighting *with* each other.' Other Brits to land themselves in hot water for fighting among themselves include Charlton pair **Mick Flanagan** and **Derek Hales** – sent off for trading punches during an FA Cup game on 9th January 1979 – and Hearts team-mates **Graeme Hogg** and **Craig Levein** who found themselves banned for ten games each after engaging in a bout of fisticuffs during a pre-season 'friendly' with Raith Rovers in 1984.

One of the strangest incidents ever to occur in a British football match took place when **Leicester City** played **Chelsea** in a League match on 18th December 1954. Defenders Stan Milburn and Jack Frogatt were officially 'credited' with half an own goal each after both attempted to clear the ball at the same time – and sent it rocketing into their own net. Oops!

Talking of own goals, consider the unfortunate case of Democrata player **Jorge Nino** in South America. Jorge wasn't the most popular man around town after he put through his own net no fewer than three times during a 5-1 defeat at the hands of Atletico Miniero.

Defenders need to be tough, hard and uncompromising, so when Finnish club Kuuysi needed a new recruit to help their cause a few years ago they recalled a player called **Eloranta** from the USA. The fierce Finn had been in great demand Stateside ... as an ice hockey star.

MAD MIDFIELDERS

They don't come much more stubborn than ex-**St.Mirren** midfielder Willie Abercromby. In 1986 Abercromby was shown the red card three times in one game. His first sending-off was for a bad tackle and he was then 'red-carded' twice more for dissent. He was fined, banned and transfer-listed – but as you'd expect he refused to leave the club and by the end of the season he had taken the 'Buddies' to Scottish Cup victory!

A similar occurrence took place in Scotland in November 1997, when **Aberdeen** striker **Dean Windass** was also dismissed three times during a match against Dundee Utd. Originally sent off for a second bookable offence, Windass then hurled a volley of abuse at referee Stewart Dougal to earn himself a second red card. His third offence was to rip out a corner flag and throw it to the ground on his way off the pitch. Windass went into the game with nine penalty points – and left it with 31! Must be something they put in the water up there.

Although the top end of the European game is awash with more money than most people would know what to do with, those in the lower reaches often struggle to rub two pennies together. In a protest at the ever-increasing cost of players, Italian clubs Polisportira and Sculese agreed an unusual transfer fee for midfielder **Guiseppe Murgi**. The player moved clubs for the princely sum of a live goat and one slice of ham. In a similar low-profile deal, when striker **Tony Cascarino** moved from non-League Crockenhill to Gillingham in 1981 his unusual transfer 'fee' amounted to 13 sets of tracksuits – not bad for a player who went on to play for the Republic of Ireland more than 70 times.

A few years ago there was a USA player who answered to the name of Bang. It wasn't his real name, he was actually called: Iron Barrel Who Slays The Buffalo With A Crack Like Thunder. Yes, he was a native American, and would have proved a commentator's nightmare. Here's a few other names that players could be called:

⚽ Often Injured Who Burps Like Thunder (Paul Gascoigne)

⚽ Appears In The Box (Ronaldo)

⚽ Orange Man Who Runs Like Lightning (Marc Overmars)

⚽ Chances With Wolves (Steve Bull)

⚽ More Sides Than A Dodecahedron (Ron Atkinson)

One of the greatest midfield players of all time he may have been, but Spain's **Luis Suarez** was nevertheless kept in the dark about his move from Inter Milan to Sampdoria in the late 1970s. Suarez knew absolutely nothing about his transfer until he read the story in a daily newspaper over his breakfast one morning. Couldn't happen now, of course. Could it?

Russian star **Streltsov** was ejected from his country's World Cup squad of 1958 to serve a prison sentence of 12 years. He returned to action in 1967, having earned some remission, and was voted the country's 'Footballer of the Year' in his first season back.

TV BREAK

Long before satellite television came along, Mexican TV was covering 'live' football several times a week. Indeed, the main station had such a hold on the game that referees were often forced to hold up games for several minutes at a time while TV reporters held impromptu interviews on the pitch.

STRANGE STRIKERS

The goalscorers are often the real stars of the side, with fame and fortune beckoning for the finest exponents of the art of hitting the net with the ball. There have been many superb strikers down the years, but few can match top Turkish hit-man **Sukur Hakan** in terms of popularity.

Sukur is such a star in his home country that when he was married his wedding was shown 'live' on national television … for *six hours!*

During a game between **Atlanta** and **Colo-Colo** in Chile the Atlanta goal-king, Vasquez, was injured and the crowd fell silent when they realised how serious it was as the stretcher-bearers ran on to carry off their hero. They didn't stay quiet for too long though, as the ambulancemen ran off in different directions and dumped the luckless Vasquez back on the ground.

Bulgarian soccer fan Kiril Donev was so besotted with his football heroes, strikers **Hristo Stoichkov** and **Petar**

Hubchev, that he offered his local monastery £3,250 to 'arrange' for the players to become saints. He even offered to double the money if the monastery would have his heroes painted on its walls.

Argentinian star **Claudio Caniggia** – who was once pictured passionately snogging Diego Maradona after scoring a goal – achieved fame as much for his long blond hair as his soccer skills, and it was no accident. In his early playing days, Claudio had short, dark hair, but he wanted to get noticed so he grew it long and dyed it. It certainly got him noticed by Maradona!

Legendary Brazilian striker **Roberto Rivelino** was famed for the power and accuracy of his shooting, and never was it better shown than when he was playing for Corinthians in a League match against Rio Preto. As soon as the ref blew for kick-off, Rivelino looked up to see that the Rio Preto 'keeper, Joachim Isadore, was still saying his pre-match prayers. So Rivelino simply blasted the ball over the goalie's head and in!

When Tottenham and England striker **Les Ferdinand** was just starting out on his career he was sent on loan to Turkish side Besiktas. To celebrate his arrival the Turks sacrificed a goat on the pitch and daubed its blood on Ferdinand's forehead and boots to bring him luck.

QUESTION

Many regard Edson Arantes do Nascimento as the greatest player of all time, but who is he, and why was he unable to sign for the world's best club of the time, Real Madrid?

Answer: Edson is rather better known as Pele and when Madrid came calling for his signature after his outstanding performances in the 1958 World Cup the Brazilian Congress declared the youngster an 'official national treasure', forbidding his sale or trade overseas!

You could have forgiven Darlington striker **Gary Innes** for getting confused during the 1996/97 season – the wandering forward played for 10 teams inside 12 months! He represented a number of Schools Rep sides before joining Sheffield United as a trainee and playing for England U18s. Gary was then released by United and moved to Darlington, from where he went on trial at Middlesbrough and loan to Waterford in Ireland before finally signing for Gateshead. Phew.

MUDDLED MANAGERS

Madcap manager **John Beck** took Cambridge United to the brink of promotion to English football's top flight in 1992 – when they lost a Play-Off Semi-Final to Leicester City – but he won few friends on the way. Among the many strange things he introduced to the Abbey Stadium were forcing his players to have cold showers before games 'to help them concentrate better' and refusing to cut the grass in the corners of the pitch so that long balls pumped forward by his team were less likely to go out of play. Still, he can't have upset that many players, because when he became boss at Preston in 1992 he took no fewer than nine United stars with him!

When the USA were playing in their first World Cup finals, in 1930, their coach had to be carried off the pitch on a stretcher. He had rushed on to help an injured player, tripped over and smashed a bottle of chloroform he had been carrying. The fumes knocked him out!

CRAZY CHAIRMEN

At most clubs it is the players who make the headlines – but at Carlisle United it's often their chairman, **Michael Knighton**, who is in the news. Before taking over at

Brunton Park, Knighton was on the board at Manchester United and celebrated joining the club by dressing up in the team strip and running out juggling a football before a League match. At Carlisle – who he promised to take from the Third Division to the Premiership in ten years – Knighton revealed that he had once been abducted by aliens in a UFO. Maybe that's what he meant by finding players in space!

Many football people have got other hobbies, and for **Atletico Madrid** president, Jesus Gil, that pastime seems to be sacking managers. At the last count, the Spanish giants have had no fewer than 32 managers in the last ten years. Gil, not renowned for his skills as a diplomat, once described his former star striker – and Mexican national hero – Hugo Sanchez as 'about as welcome here as a piranha in a bidet'.

FANTASTIC FOOTBALL FAMILIES

Manchester United's **Neville** brothers have won many headlines in recent years – but it shouldn't come as too much of a surprise, the pair hail from a successful sporting family. Not only is their sister, Tracey, an England netball international, but she also works at Bury ... as does their mum, dad – called Neville Neville – auntie, uncle and cousin!

How do you think TV commentator John Motson would handle this one? When Greek giants Olympiakos were founded in the mid-1920s their five-man forward line were all brothers by the name of **Andrianopoulos**.

There have been several cases of brothers turning out on the same side, with the most famous probably being the **Charltons**, Bobby and Jack, who each represented England in the 1966 World Cup Final.

Three brothers have lined-up together on at least three occasions. The most recent time was in September 1989, when Danny **Wallace** (24) was joined by his 19-year-old

twin brothers Rodney and Ray for Southampton in a First Division match. Other famous threesomes have included: William, John and George **Carr** (all Middlesbrough, 1920-23); Sam, James and Jack **Tonner** (all Clapton Orient, 1919/20).

The first father and son to appear in the same team in an English League game were Alec (39) and David **Herd** (17), who played for Stockport County in a Division Three (North) game against Hartlepool in 1951. Alec was the player-manager, and he brought son David on as a substitute. Ian **Bowyer** (39) and son Gary (18) appeared together for Hereford Utd at Scunthorpe in Division Four on 21st April 1990.

Iceland made football history when they beat Estonia 3-0 in Tallin in 1996. Arnar **Gudjohnsen** (35) started the match, but was replaced after 62 minutes by his 17-year-old son Eidur. This was the first time that a father and son had appeared in the same international match.

In September 1996, 21-year-old Nick **Scaife**, of Bishop Auckland, faced his father, Bobby (41), of Pickering Town, in an FA Cup Qualifying game. It was the first time that father and son had lined up on opposite sides in a senior match.

And you can quote me on that ...
'Great. Tell him he's Pele.' Partick Thistle manager John Lambie on being told that his striker, Colin McGlashan, had been struck on the

ALL HAIL ROBERTO!

Lazio fans gave Roberto di Matteo quite a send-off when he announced he was quitting the Rome club to join Chelsea — they stoned his car. Believe it or not it was a gesture of affection. Just imagine what they do if they are annoyed with a player.

head and couldn't remember who he was.

In most northern European nations, the weather has a big say in exactly when and where games can be played and in many countries there is a mid-season break built in to prevent the worst excesses of the winter disrupting the season too much. However in Britain no such arrangement is made – and for at least one player a sudden snowfall was more than just a chilly shock. Way back in 1956 **Peterborough United** had on trial a 25-year-old Nigerian forward called Jesilimi Balogun. While playing for the Reserves one Saturday afternoon in November it began to snow and Jesilimi, who had never experienced snow before, was so terrified that he ran off the pitch and into the changing-rooms. He refused to step back outside until the snow had stopped falling. Although he never made the first team at Peterborough, Jesilimi did go on to play senior football with Queen's Park Rangers.

One of the favourite comments made by managers when supporters or newspaper folk try to point out shortcomings in their side is that such people 'know nothing about the game'. In some cases this may well be true, but few observers could stifle their giggles at an event which took place at The Dell in November 1996. Former Liverpool and Rangers boss **Graeme Souness** – then manager at Premiership **Southampton** – couldn't believe his ears when 'World Footballer of the Year' George Weah telephoned him to recommend a player to the Saints. He'd have probably been better not believing them! The caller said that Ali Dia, a former Senegalese international and ex-Paris St.Germain striker was available on a free transfer and desperately wanted to play in England. Souness, always on the look-out for a bargain, promptly snapped up Dia – after all, what better person than the 'World Footballer of the Year' to get a reference from? The only slight problem was that, well, it wasn't George Weah on the phone. When Matt Le Tissier was injured playing against Leeds, Dia was sent on to substitute for him – and it was immediately obvious that the new boy was completely out of his depth. It turned out that Souness had signed a former French First Division reserve! Oops.

NATIONAL IDENTITY?

Oyvind Larsen, assistant coach of Norway's national side, once compiled a dossier of the different ways the other countries in the world played football, in an attempt to work out their weaknesses. He came to the conclusion that Germans play with their brains, the English play with their hearts and the Brazilians play with their hips. Presumably, when South Africa were banned from competitive international sport due to their government's racist 'apartheid' policy, they played with themselves. Larsen failed to mention what the Italians played with.

QUESTION

What was unusual about Wolves' keeper Mike Stowell's trip to Algeria for an England 'B' international in December 1990?

FANTASTIC FOOTBALL FAUX PAS!

Newcastle United goalkeeper Shay Given must have wanted the ground to open up and swallow him during a game against Coventry City in November 1997. Given, a highly-rated Republic of Ireland international, had done well to catch a high ball into his area despite the close attentions of a couple of Coventry players. But when the young 'keeper decided to roll the ball along the ground before booting it clear he should have taken the precaution of looking over his shoulder first. Coventry striker Dion Dublin had been lurking off the pitch and he quickly sprinted past the surprised Given to tap the ball into the empty net. The match finished 2-2, and left Given with a red face.

QUESTION

Leeds goalkeeper Gary Sprake features in one of the most commonly seen 'football funnies' of all time. Why?

Answer: Sprake, who was one of the best goalkeepers of his era, was playing for Leeds against Liverpool in the 1970s when disaster struck. He went to throw the ball out to a defender, but he got mixed up and released the ball too late – throwing it straight into his own goal!

Answer: He made part of it in a snow plough. Severe snow storms in the West Midlands meant that Mike had to hire the snow-clearing machine to get him to the airport in time to catch his flight to North Africa.

NATURAL PERFORMERS

One of the biggest footballing attractions in Spain is a team called Las Ibericas. They are a side composed entirely of Spanish actresses. They joined forces originally for a film in which they appeared as a women's football team – and enjoyed the experience so much they kept the side going.

FANTASTIC FOOTBALL FLASHBACK

As Britain lurches through the Industrial Revolution, the popularity of football begins to grow all over the kingdom during a time of immense economic and political change.

The first 'proper' steam railway line is officially opened in 1825 – linking Stockton and Darlington in the north east of England, and five years later the famous Liverpool–Manchester line is introduced. It becomes easier for people – and therefore footballers – to travel around the country, moving their skills and ideas from place to place.

These early days also pave the way for British Rail's 'Football Special' trains of many years later. Due to Britain's snobby 'class' system, there are three ways to travel on the trains – first class (the height of luxury, perfect for club chairmen, FA executives), second class (seats, but no roof, for club directors), open class (packed in tight and open to the elements for players, supporters and everyone else). There are no prizes for guessing which model was later re-introduced for football fans!

Ruler throughout this period is Queen Victoria, who marries her teutonic cousin Albert in 1840, thus securing the first tie between England and Germany. Happily, it doesn't ever get to a shoot-out. Other principle figures of the time helping to light the way to the formation of the FA, include the lady of the lamp herself, Florence Nightingale, who busies herself working as physio for the players injured during the Crimean War.

In 1837, the very public humiliation of placing people in the stocks – where passers-by come along to hurl abuse, as well as other things, at the victim – is banned. A similar form of punishment could soon be introduced with news that FIFA (Federation Internationale de Football Association) are considering the introduction of video playbacks of controversial refereeing decisions.

1823 This is a very important date for football lovers. At Rugby School, some nutter called William Webb Ellis got a bit bored during a game one day and decided to pick up the ball and run with it. Everybody said it was unfair, but there were no rules, so William just carried on. Ellis had started the split between 'rugger' and 'soccer'.

1848 Fourteen smarty-pants from Cambridge University got together to write the first set of football rules so that schools and universities could actually play against each other. Unfortunately, not everybody agreed with the new rules – so what's new?

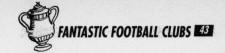

Cambridge Rules

Here are some of the rules that the Cambridge guys drew up...

① The goalposts had to be 8 yards (7.3 metres) apart, but could be as high as you wanted. Even the *biggest hoofer in school couldn't have missed in those days!*

② To score you had to kick the ball between the posts. *OK, maybe they could.*

③ Every time a goal was scored, the teams changed ends. *Talk about confusing!*

④ Any player was allowed to catch the ball, but you weren't able to run with it in your hands.

⑤ You weren't allowed to pick the ball up off the ground, or to throw it to another player.

⑥ You were only allowed to pass the ball backwards, and if you were in front of the ball you were considered 'off-side' and not allowed to touch it.

⑦ You weren't allowed to kick, trip, hack, hold or push an opponent. *Or chop their head off and use it as a ball, for that matter.*

1855 Sheffield FC, the world's oldest football club, was formed and matches allowed to take place on the Sheffield Cricket Ground at Bramall Lane. The question is: if they were the only club, who did they play against?

1863 The Football Association (FA) was formed and the first widely accepted Laws of the Game were drawn up.

1865 To stop games ending up at 150-all, a piece of string or tape was introduced, to join the posts together at 8 feet (2.4m) high. *Time for the hoofer to stop playing again.*

1867 Offside and only one goalkeeper per team introduced. This was to stop the clubs of the day playing six goalkeepers and five goal-hangers up front. Trouble was, the player nearest the goal-line was deemed to be the goalkeeper – so anybody could save the ball and then say they were in goal.

1872 First FA Cup Final played, at Kennington Oval (where England get beaten at cricket by Australia these days). Wanderers beat Royal Engineers 1-0 with a goal by Morton Peto Betts, who was named after the man who designed Nelson's Column in London.

FANTASTIC FOOTBALL FELLOW!

The star player in the early days of football was a bloke called the Honourable Arthur Kinnaird, who was described as: 'without doubt the best player of the day.' He played in 11 FA Cup Finals (won five) and was renowned for being a bit of a hard nut. Arthur – who was a lot less honourable than his name suggested – was a big fan of 'hacking' (duffing people up during the game) and his Mum was so concerned that she once said: 'I'm afraid he will one day come home with a broken leg.' But a friend put her mind at rest. 'Don't worry,' he said. 'If he does it will not be his own.'

3 FANTASTIC FOOTBALL FACTS AND FIGURES

GREAT GOALSCORERS

Top score by a single player in a first-class match in Britain is 13 goals. It was a fellow called **John Petrie** who did the damage, as his club, Arbroath, trounced Bon Accord 36-0 in the Scottish Cup First Round on 12th September 1885. The match score also remains a record. Players of the old Dundee Harp side must have been cursing their luck that afternoon. On the same day, in the same competition, Harp beat Aberdeen Rovers by a similarly whopping 35-0.

England striker **Vivian Woodward** was clearly a class goal-getter. He scored seven against France in an Amateur international (won 15-0) on 1st November 1906, and then followed that up by grabbing six vs Holland (won 9-1) on 11th December 1909.

SWEET SMELL OF SUCCESS?

There is a fad in Spain for players to try and bring themselves luck by planting a clove of garlic behind the goal. Some grounds are starting to look like they have an allotment at each end!

One of the most important single goals of all time could be said to have been scored by Germany's **Oliver Bierhoff**. Brought on as a substitute in the 1996 European Championship Final at Wembley, Bierhoff scored in the 95th minute to settle the match in 'sudden death' extra-time.

The first British match to be decided by 'sudden death' was in the 1994/95 Auto Windscreen Shield, when Huddersfield's **Iain Dunn** netted after 107 minutes to defeat Lincoln City. The Final of that year's competition was settled in the same fashion, **Paul Tait** doing the business for Birmingham City against Carlisle after 103 minutes.

While those goals were undoubtedly vital, there can have been few more controversial than **Geoff Hurst's** second, and England's third, in the 1966 World Cup Final. Hurst's shot on the turn crashed off the crossbar and bounced down – but which side of the line did it fall? After a long consultation between Swiss referee Mr Dienst and Russian linesman Tofik Bakhramov the goal was given. Hurst placed the game beyond doubt a few minutes later by completing his hat-trick and putting England 4-2 up, but controversy remains to this day. Unfortunately for West Ham striker Hurst, he was unable to celebrate his historic hat-trick with the traditional prize of the matchball. German defender Helmut Haller quietly stuffed it up the front of his shirt in all the confusion as England celebrated … and took it home with him!

Brazilian legend **Pele** is widely recognised as the world's greatest ever player, but it is easy to forget sometimes just how important he was to the sides he played for. His record reads 1,282 goals scored in 1,365 matches played for Brazil and his club side, Santos, however many of those were in friendlies. His 1,000th goal was a penalty against Vasco de Gama, in the Maracana Stadium, Rio de Janeiro, on 19th November 1969. To give an idea of his skills, take the 1959 season as an example. That year the 19-year-old Pele scored an astonishing 126 goals for Santos and Brazil. He played in

103 games and scored in 69 of them, hitting 17 hat-tricks in the process.

NATIONAL DISGRACE

With all the new nations formed following the collapse of the old communist bloc countries, nations could be excused for not being overly-familiar with the national anthems of some of their opponents. But when two of the world's oldest established countries do battle on the football field you'd think it would be alright. Not so when China played a Greece XI recently. As is the tradition, the teams lined up before kick-off and stood to attention for the national anthems. The Greeks politely stood for what they thought was the Chinese anthem, and the Chinese stood for what they believed was the Greek anthem. It was actually the new theme music for a toothpaste advert, played by mistake.

The highest score ever recorded in a World Cup Qualifying game was Iran's 17-0 victory away to The Maldives on 2nd June 1997. The team from the tiny island in the Indian Ocean did improve though – they only lost the return tie 9-0. In the finals series the biggest winning margin is shared between three matches: Hungary 10, El Salvador 1 (15.06.82); Hungary 9, South Korea 0 (17.06.54); Yugoslavia 9, Zaire 0 (18.06.74).

Everton's **William 'Dixie' Dean** – a nickname he hated – created an English League scoring record in 1927/28 which is unlikely ever to be beaten. The powerful front man scored 60 times in 39 First Division matches. For good measure, he also netted three times in FA Cup ties and 19 in representative games, taking his tally for the season to 82. The League record was previously held by Middlesbrough's George Camsell, with 59 goals in 37 Second Division matches the previous year.

QUESTION

Here's a look at the top scorers for each of the 'home' countries. Can you match up the players with their countries and their totals?

Frank Stapleton	Scotland	49
Colin Clarke	Wales	30
Denis Law	England	28
Ian Rush	N. Ireland	13
Kenny Dalglish	Rep Ireland	30
Bobby Charlton	Scotland	20

QUESTION

Which player scored seven goals in a game, and still ended up on the losing side?

Answer: Denis Law: He scored six for Man City in an FA Cup Fourth Round tie at Luton in January 1961, but none of them counted as the match was abandoned due to a waterlogged pitch. City lost the replay 3–1, with that man Law scoring again.

Answers: Frank Stapleton, Rep Ireland, 20; Colin Clarke, N Ireland, 13; Denis Law, Scotland, 30; Ian Rush, Wales, 28; Kenny Dalglish, Scotland, 30; Bobby Charlton, England, 49.

The major international tournaments have witnessed some remarkable scoring exploits down the years, but the honours for best individual performances go to two Frenchmen. **Juste Fontaine** scored a remarkable 13 World Cup finals goals at Sweden in 1958 – not bad considering he was only a reserve at the start of the tournament. Three-times European Footballer of the Year **Michel Platini** netted 11 European Championship goals in France in 1984.

The fastest international goal was scored by San Marino's **Davide Gaultieri**. Following a mistake from England's Stuart Pearce, Gaultieri pounced after just 8.3 seconds to put the tiny mountain-top state 1-0 up in a World Cup Qualifier in Bologna on 17th November 1993. England recovered from that early shock to win the match 7-1. Denmark's **John Jensen** scored five seconds after coming on as a substitute against Belgium in a European Championship Qualifier on 12th October 1994.

At the World Cup tournament proper, the fastest recorded strike was by Czechoslovakia's **Vaclav Masek**, against Mexico in Chile in the 1962 finals, after just 15 seconds. England's **Bryan Robson** scored in 27 seconds vs France at Spain 1982.

And talking of quick, **Tottenham** scored 4 goals in just four minutes, 44 seconds, at home to Southampton on 7th February 1993 (won 4-2), while Liverpool's **Robbie Fowler** netted a four-and-a-half minute hat-trick against Arsenal on 28th August 1994 (won 3-0).

PROMISING START!

If you've ever turned up late for a game for whatever reason – missed the bus, couldn't find anywhere to park the car, little brother got run over – then you will appreciate the shock felt by those arriving after the kick-off of a game between Independiente and Gimnasia in an Argentinian League match in March 1973. Normally you'd expect to shuffle along to your seat and then say to the person next you: 'Anything much happened?', knowing that the answer will be "No, not really." But just imagine if one time the reply was: 'Yes, the opposition are 3-0 up.' You'd never believe it, but that's what happened to Gimnasia fans that afternoon, as striker Magiloni stuck three goals past their team in the first one minute and 50 seconds.

Several goalkeepers have found the opposition net down the years, generally from long clearances or via the penalty spot. But Manchester United's Danish international **Peter Schmeichel** went one better in the 1995/96 UEFA Cup. With United 2-1 down on the night, Schmeichel went forward for a corner and headed an improbable 89th minute equaliser against Russia's Rotor Volograd. It was to no avail, though, as United still went out on away goals.

United's old adversaries, and England's most successful club, **Liverpool** set a Football League record with eight different scorers when beating **Crystal Palace** 9-0 in a First

Division match on 12th September 1989. Steve Nicol (2), Steve McMahon, Ian Rush, Gary Gillespie, Peter Beardsley, John Aldridge, John Barnes and Glenn Hysen all found the net. Seven months later Palace gained ample revenge, however, beating the Anfield club 4-3 in a thrilling FA Cup Semi-Final at Villa Park.

West Ham defender Alvin Martin scored an unlikely hat-trick in April 1986, when he netted his goals against three different 'keepers. Newcastle's regular No.1 Martin Thomas injured a shoulder early on and was replaced between the sticks by first Chris Hedworth and then Peter Beardsley. West Ham ran out comfortable 8-1 winners that night.

At the other end of the field are the men whose job is to keep the ball out of the net. The world record for not conceding a goal is held by Atletico Madrid goalkeeper **Abel Resino** in the 1990/91 campaign. Resino went an astonishing 1,275 minutes without being beaten. In international football that record is held by legendary Italian

Dino Zoff who put up the shutters for Italy for a total of 1,142 minutes between September 1972 and June 1974. It was the unlikely figure of Hamilton Academicals' **Adrian Sprott** who brought to an end the British clean-sheet record. Prior to his goal, scored on 31st January 1987, Rangers' 'keeper **Chris Woods** had remained unbeaten for 1,196 minutes.

Their 'no-goal' records wouldn't have been unduly threatened by the following two clubs. In the English Premiership, **Crystal Palace** hold the unwanted distinction of going a mind-numbing nine consecutive games without scoring, between October 1994 and January 1995. Even that dismal spell, though, is not the worst in Britain. **Stirling Albion** managed to play 14 matches in a row between January and August 1981 without once troubling the goalkeeper.

CROWDED OUT

The largest paying crowd ever to have gathered to watch a match was, appropriately enough, at the final match of the 1950 World Cup tournament in Brazil. A whopping 199,850 squeezed through the turnstiles at the **Maracana Stadium** in Rio de Janeiro to see the local heroes do battle with Uruguay. They didn't get the result they were looking for, though, as Uruguay won the match 2-1.

In England, the biggest official crowd was the 126,047 who paid to be at **Wembley** for the grand old stadium's first ever match, the 1923 FA Cup Final between Bolton and West Ham. Despite assertions in the matchday programme that everybody in the purpose-built new ground would have a good view, eye-witnesses estimated that between 150,000 and 200,000 fans forced their way into the stadium and police – led by a famous white horse called Billy – spent an age clearing the pitch before the game could kick-off. Even then, hundreds of supporters were left simply standing by the touchlines as there was nowhere else for them to go. Billy the police horse became a legend in his own right after his calm display, although Hammers coach Charlie Paynter tried to blame hoofprints for his team's defeat!

Until its recent refurbishment, **Hampden Park** in Scotland was one of the world's biggest stadiums. It boasts two European attendance records, with 135,826 present for the 1970 European Cup Semi-Final between Celtic and Leeds Utd, and 127,621 in the ground for the 1960 European Cup Final between Real Madrid and Eintracht Frankfurt.

FULL HOUSE

There was a serious case of overcrowding when Ghanaian international star Alain Gouamane's performance earned him a bonus of £40,000 and a new house. Under the terms of the prize he had to share it with his relatives, which meant he had to cram 30 other people under his new roof – and give them £1,290 each.

ON THE INTERNATIONAL FRONT

When world football's governing body, FIFA, was formed way back in 1904 it had just seven members: Belgium, Denmark, France, Holland, Spain, Sweden and Switzerland. It now boasts almost 200 countries.

QUESTION

Here's a quick look at five of the world's most capped international players. But can you match up the players with the countries they represented?

Majid Abdullah (157 caps):	Germany
Thomas Ravelli (139):	N. Ireland
Peter Shilton (125):	Saudi Arabia
Lothar Matthaus (122):	Sweden
Pat Jennings (119):	England

Brazil succeeded **Hungary** as holders of the longest unbeaten run in international football. Their incredible tally reached 37 games – including 30 victories – between December 1993 and January 1996, before they finally lost to Mexico in the CONCACAF Gold Cup Final. Poor Hungary had gone 32 matches undefeated, and lost only once over a period of several years – but that match was the 1954 World Cup Final against West Germany.

Believe it or not, several players have turned out as senior internationals for more than one country, including:

Johnny Carey:	Rep of Ireland (29 caps) and N. Ireland (7)
Ferenc Puskas:	Hungary (84) and Spain (4)
Alfredo di Stefano:	Argentina (7) and Spain (31)
Ladislav Kubala:	Hungary (3), Czechoslovakia (11) and Spain (19)

INDUSTRIAL REVOLUTIONS

Pakistan is not exactly one of the world powers of soccer, yet it can lay claim to being one of the most important countries on the football atlas. Why? The little town of Sialkot is responsible for 85 per cent of all the world's footballs, making 40 million a year. It all started when some British soldiers in the Punjab late last century went to a local shoemaker to have their leather football repaired. A whole new industry was founded.

YOUNGEST AND OLDEST

Age, it seems, is no barrier to becoming a footballer. Whether you are just out of nappies or about to call on the services of 'Zimmer Frames-R-Us', you can still strut your stuff on the football field.

Up in Scotland, goalkeeper **Ronnie Simpson** was just 14 years, 304 days-old when he played his first game for Queen's Park in 1945, while defender **Andy Awford** (now Portsmouth) represented Worcester City in the FA Cup at 15 years, 88 days.

Jason Dozzell was still a pupil at Chantry High School in Ipswich when he came on as a sub for his local club in a game against Coventry City on 4th February 1984 – and scored. Jason remains the youngest player, at 16 years, 57 days, to have scored a top-flight goal in England.

Mind you, it will surprise few people that **Alan Shearer** celebrated his senior debut for Southampton, against Arsenal on 9th April 1988, with a hat-trick aged just 17 years, 240 days, making him the youngest player to achieve that particular feat. Shearer has, in fact, scored on his debut for every team at every level he has played.

On the international front, the youngest player ever to appear in the World Cup finals is **Norman Whiteside**. Northern Ireland international Whiteside was 17 years, 42 days, when he represented his country vs Yugoslavia in Spain on 17th June 1982 – making him a full 195 days younger than the previous record holder, **Pele**. Just for good measure, Whiteside is also N. Ireland's youngest international and the youngest Wembley scorer (for Man Utd vs Liverpool, League Cup Final, aged 17 years, 324 days).

The youngest player to score a goal in a senior international is believed to be Sierra Leone's **Mohamed Kallon**, who was a mere 15 years, 6 months and 15 days when he found the net in an African Nations Cup match against Congo on 22nd April 1995.

But if those players were making waves as youngsters, it appears that the passing of time does nothing to dim the desire to lace up your boots …

It is well known that the legendary **Stanley Matthews** was still playing top flight League football in England past his 50th birthday. His final game for Stoke City came against Fulham on 6th February 1965, when he was a ripe old 50 years and 5 days. But, believe it or not, Matthews is not the oldest player to have turned out in a Football League match. That honour falls to New Brighton manager **Neil McBain** who was an ancient 52 years, 4 months when he was pressed into service as an emergency goalkeeper for a Division Three (North) match against Hartlepool on 15th March 1957.

It's all very well finishing your career as an old man – but how about starting it as one. New boy **Andrew Cunningham** made his League debut for Newcastle, against Leicester City in the old First Division, on 2nd February 1929. He was aged a spritely 38 years, 2 days.

The oldest British international player is **Billy Meredith**, who played for Wales against England on 15th March 1920 aged 45 years, 229 days, while **Leslie Compton** made his international debut for England, against Wales on 15th November 1950, when he was 32 years, 2 months old. Leslie was also a successful county cricketer with Middlesex.

SPOILED FOR CHOICE

Not many people turn down the chance to play for their country in the World Cup, but in 1973 New Zealand star Vic Pollard did just that. Instead, he chose to visit England with his country's Test cricket side, as he was also an international at the bat-and-ball game.

BIGGEST AND SMALLEST

Ask any footballer and they'll tell you – size doesn't matter either. Players have come in all shapes and sizes over the years: fat, thin, tall or small, it's not important. So long as you can play, of course.

And you can quote me on that ...
'I don't care if a player's a martian. If he can score me 25 goals a season I'll take him. If he only wants £400 a week, even better.' Dave Bassett, then manager of Sheffield Utd, 1994.

Being tall, for example, can be a great help if you are a goalkeeper. Early this century, Notts County had a whopping great 'keeper called **Albert Iremonger**, who measured up at 6ft 5in, which is the same size as current West Ham and Canada stopper **Craig Forrest** and Derby's

Estonian international **Mart Poom**. However, the tallest player around is not a goalkeeper but a goalscorer – Oxford United's gigantic Kevin Francis, who is an astonishing 6ft 7in tall.

> ### And you can quote me on that ...
> *'To be fair he's got quite a good touch, but he's quite daunting. If I ever need my guttering fixed I'll give him a call.'* Then QPR midfielder Ray Wilkins after playing against Kevin Francis.

So this is what they mean by the big League!

Don't panic if you are a bit of a shorty, though, there could still be a place for you in soccer's hall of fame. **Bobby Kerr** was the captain of Sunderland's historic FA Cup-winning side which beat mighty Leeds in 1973 ... and he stood at only 5ft 4in in his little stockinged feet. And several players have gone on to greater things after being dismissed by clubs for their size. Internationals **Kevin Keegan**, **Alan Ball** and **Gordon Strachan**, for example, were all originally told they were 'too small' to make it as professional footballers.

OK, so now we know that height isn't vital – what about weight?

Well, one of the most famous players of all time was the goalkeeper **William 'Fatty' Foulke**, who played for Sheffield United and Chelsea back in the early days of the game. Fatty weighed in at a scales-busting 22 stones in his heydey, that's more than seven stones heavier than lofty Kevin Francis!

Elsewhere, famous Scotsman **Patsy Gallagher**, who was a hero for Celtic fans in the early 20th century, hardly bothered the weighing machine at all at little over seven stones. Even famous skinnies of today like **Steve McManaman** (10st 6lb) would be able to squash Patsy.

FANTASTIC FOOTBALL FIRSTS

Of course, back in the mists of time, somebody had to be the first to achieve …

Up in Scotland, Premier Division **Aberdeen** can lay claim to a number of historic 'firsts'. In the 1920s their famous Pittodrie Stadium was the site of the first ever 'dug-outs' for the manager and his coaches. Donald Coleman requested the constructions be put into place so that he could get closer to the action and examine his players' fancy footwork. Pittodrie was formerly a dung-heap used by the local police and the name itself is loosely translated from Gaelic and means: 'place of manure'. Despite being a pile of *@!*, Pittodrie became Britain's first all-seater stadium in 1978.

You couldn't see it happening today, but Liverpool's **Alex Raisbeck** regularly turned out for the Reds whilst wearing a pair of glasses – the first player to prove that four eyes were better than two. It obviously didn't affect his performances too much, as he managed to make almost 350 appearances for the Anfield club during his 11-year career there. Another player to make a spectacle of himself while playing was a **J. Jurion**, who was capped 49 times for Belgium and wore glasses throughout his career.

The first time **numbered cards** were used in the Football League, to inform players they were due to be substituted, was in 1975. Even back then the players developed temporary blindness when their number was displayed, and, when finally forced to recognise that their time was up, pointed at themselves mouthing 'what me?' and ran off shaking their heads.

After an impeccable start to his career as national manager, and a perfect World Cup campaign, **Glenn Hoddle** saw his England side lose 1-0 at home to Italy in February 1997, thanks to a goal from pint-sized Chelsea striker Gianfranco Zola. It was the first time England had lost a World Cup Qualifier on their own turf. In the return match in October of the same year England held Italy to a 0-0 draw in Rome: the first time the Italians had failed to win a World Cup qualifier in the eternal city.

And you can quote me on that ...
'I hear Glenn's found God. That must have been one hell of a pass.' Comedian Jasper Carrott on the news that England boss Glenn Hoddle had become a 'born-again' Christian.

Berwick Rangers have the distinction of being the first and only English club to play their football in the Scottish League. Formed in 1881 the border town team began as members of the Northumberland Football Association, but joined the Scottish League in 1951 – and have stayed there ever since.

Steaua Bucharest, of Romania, became the first 'eastern bloc' country to lift the European Cup when they defeated Barcelona 2-0 in a frankly rather pathetic penalty shoot-out – but there was more to the club than met the eye. Personally supported by the country's all-powerful leader, Nicolai Ceaucescu, Steaua were given the automatic right to sign any players they wanted from any other club in the country.

After his ancestors had all turned their backs on football, **King George V** became the first reigning monarch to attend an FA Cup Final when he turned up at Crystal Palace in 1914 to see Burnley beat Liverpool 1-0. One of the League's founding clubs, Burnley have reached the Final on two other occasions – 1947 and 1962 – finishing runners-up both times.

Although floodlights weren't officially invented until 1955, Scottish giants **Celtic** were the first club to see the light and try playing after dark. On Christmas Day 1893 they rigged up lamps on poles all around the sidelines, and had others suspended on wires above the pitch, as they entertained Clyde.

In 1995 the tiny European state of **Luxembourg** finally won a competitive fixture – its first such success since 1980 ending a run of more than 80 matches without victory. That sequence had brought with it two more unwanted records – 32 consecutive defeats and failing to score in nine successive international matches. As is the way with these things, Luxembourg's 1-0 triumph in Malta was swiftly followed by two more successes: 1-0 vs Czech Republic (h) and 1-0 vs Malta (h).

RINGING THE CHANGES

Sick and tired of the excuses your club manager comes up with for losing games? Well try this one for size. Spanish First Division side Logrones put the blame for a string of defeats on ... mobile phones. Coach Liber Arispe banned the use of mobile phones by his players because they were constantly being phoned up during training and while they were on the bench during matches. The press kept phoning them for quotes during games.

AND FINALLY...

The list of merchandise available at football clubs becomes longer and more bizarre as the years go by. What began with simple scarves and hats soon expanded into replica shirts and on to items like key-fobs, window stickers, baby-grows and even ladies underwear. In more recent years, milk cartons in club colours have hit the shelves at many stadiums, while supporters at Borussia Dortmund in Germany have for some time been able to purchase branded sausages. Now undertakers in Germany have jumped on the bandwagon – or should that be hearse? – of producing football-related goods. The men in black have hit on a novel idea for fans wishing to show their ever-lasting loyalty to their clubs. Supporters can now be buried in coffins bearing the colours and emblems of their favourite clubs.

Sounds like a good idea, especially if you follow Bury.

All of these records needed to be broken somewhere, and for many fans a club's ground is the most important place on earth.

Some teams boast magnificent stadia with state-of-the-art facilites and the very best that money can buy. Others don't.

In the next chapter we'll take a look at some of the places that football calls home … But first …

On and off the football field, other European nations begin nibbling at British heels, with the Belgians, in particular, beginning to 'scout' the best African talent, starting with the Congo.

Suitably worried, Britain invade what is now South Africa and kick off the bloody Boer War, which results

in thousands of deaths and a public relations own goal for Britian's already murky reputation abroad.

Meanwhile, back at home education is made free for all – or for all those who could afford not to work anyway – and the infamous Jack the Ripper begins his reign of terror, which results in the murder of at least ten prostitutes in London.

Future transfer dealings – and phone calls to Asian 'betting syndicates' – are made significantly easier as Alexander Graham Bell invents the first telephone in 1876. There is no chance of a wrong number, either – he owns the only one.

1873 Scottish FA formed. At last … now England would have someone to play.

1874 Kicking the opposition will never be as much fun again, as shinpads are invented by a fellow called Sam Widdowson, who plays for Nottingham Forest and England.

1878 The referee's whistle is heard for the first time, in a game between Nottingham Forest and Sheffield Norfolk. Before this, referees simply had to shout their instructions.

1883 Wooden crossbars introduced. The trouble with string or tape was that goalkeepers could pull it out of the way at crucial times – and also, if the ball hit the string nobody knew if it was a goal or not. The new rule stopped them cheating quite so much.

Portsmouth officials were embarrassed in November 1989 when a visiting Danish referee, officiating in a youth international, discovered that one of the Fratton Park crossbars was an inch too low.

1885 Players allowed to become professional, and get paid for the first time.

1888 Football League founded.

THE ORIGINAL DOZEN

Here's how results went on the first ever day of the Football League, 8th September 1888.

Bolton	3	Derby	6
Everton	2	Accrington	1
Preston	5	Burnley	2
Stoke	0	WBA	2
Wolves	1	Aston Villa	1

The other two founder members, Blackburn and Notts County, had a late kick-off – a week late. They played their first games on September 15th:

Blackburn	5	Accrington	5
Everton	2	Notts Co	1

Give me a four, no make that a five, no...

PRESTON vs HYDE

QUESTION

Which one of the 'Original Dozen' clubs is no longer in the League?

It was Preston's repeated hammerings of all-comers – such as their famous 26-0 win over Hyde in the FA Cup in 1887 – which persuaded Scotsman William McGregor to convince critics that the formation of the Football League was a good idea. He said that it would lead to a 'greater spread of talent and make the game more popular around the country' – and he was proved right ... eventually. But in the League's first season Preston – nicknamed 'The Invincibles' – lived up to their name. They won the League with 40 points out of a possible 44, scoring 74 goals and conceding just 15. They also won the Cup without conceding a single goal. They were rubbish the following season – they lost four whole times on their way to winning the League again!

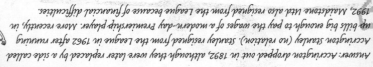

Answer: Accrington dropped out in 1892, although they were later replaced by a side called Accrington Stanley (no relation). Stanley resigned from the League in 1962 after running up bills big enough to pay the wages of a modern-day Premiership player. More recently, in 1992, Maidstone Utd also resigned from the League because of financial difficulties.

4 FANTASTIC FOOTBALL GROUNDS

There's no place like home, and for football clubs home is where the ground is.

Some stadia are more interesting than the clubs that play in them, with tales of ghostly goings-on and age-old curses giving fans something to talk about when the football on display is less than *phenomenal* ...

When footballs got kicked over the Railway End terrace at **Alloa** a few years ago they sometimes ended up travelling miles. It was nothing to do with any supersonic kicking skills from The Wasps' strikers, though. The railway line used to pass so close to the terracing that stray balls would occasionally end up in the open goods trucks – and hitch a lift all the way to Perth on the east coast!

Fans who have accused **Arsenal** defender Tony Adams of playing like a donkey would be delighted to learn that the Gunners believe that a dead horse brings them good luck! The horse, which died in a construction accident during the building of Highbury, was buried under the site of what is now the North Bank. Other ghosts and ghoulies at Arsenal include the spectre of former manager Herbert Chapman, who is said to walk the corridors of his old club.

TRUE OR FALSE?

The artificial playing surface 'astroturf' was named after the Houston Astrodome, in Texas, USA?

Having moved out of the Aston area of Birmingham because of the severe competition in that district, **Aston Villa** set up home in the adjacent suburb of Perry Barr in 1876. Their new pitch had a hayrick in the middle of it which had to be removed before every game, a big hump near one goal and a cluster of trees all the way down one touchline. The players changed in a blacksmith's hut. Eventually, Villa got fed up with all the aggro at Perry Barr and moved to the site of an old amusement park called Aston Lower Grounds in 1897 – and Villa Park was born. An aquarium, skating rink and restaurant stood where the club offices now are, while the playing area is where the boating lake used to be.

During the 1950s the Main Stand at **Barnsley's** Oakwell Stadium had a pair of swing doors which led out onto the pitch. One of the players, keen to make a dramatic entrance, often charged headlong through them – until one day a team-mate reversed the hinges and the player knocked himself unconscious!

Answer: True. The first ever artificial pitch was laid there in the 1960s.

There's a case of split personalities going on down at **Chester City**, where they are in two minds about which country they are in. The club's purpose-built new Deva Stadium (completed in 1992) is constructed half in England and half in Wales. The Welsh FA made the decision for Chester – banning them from entering the Welsh Cup any more (they had previously won the competition in 1908, 1933 and 1947).

Despite being less than 100 yards apart, the grounds of **Dundee** and **Dundee United** are not the closest opposing football grounds in the world. That honour falls to Hungarian clubs **MTK** and **BKV Elore** of Budapest – their stadiums actually back onto each other!

TRUE OR FALSE?

It is a rule that football goalposts are always painted white.

If Scottish club **Dunfermline Athletic** are ever accused of shipping goals it shouldn't come as a surprise. Way back in 1935 the East Terrace at East End Park was rebuilt using wood salvaged from the famous ocean liner *Mauretania*, which was being broken up in a nearby shipyard.

During the early days of their existence, Edinburgh rivals **Hearts** and **Hibs** shared grounds at both East Meadows and Powderhall. This led to some, shall we say, intense competition between the clubs which still exists today. On one occasion, the Hearts skipper Tom Purdie was chased by a big group of Hibs fans after a match – and fought them off with a whip! Wonder if that's why they said he had a cracking shot?

Answer: True, although it's only a fairly recent Law. In the old days old posts could be painted any colour.

Now we've heard some decent excuses for calling games off over the years, but the one used by Iceland's **IB Vestmann** in 1973 tops the lot. The club's ground was sunk under a pool of lava after a volcano erupted, and was obviously made unusable. However, Vestmann were not to be denied their historic stadium and, two years later, it was dug free and used again! The managers really were sitting in a dug-out that day.

When **Middlesbrough** entertained **Burnley** in an FA Cup tie in 1947 there was an overwhelming interest in the game and thousands of fans were locked out of the ground. To keep the disappointed supporters happy the city's Chief Constable stood on the wall surrounding the pitch and gave the listening crowd a running commentary of events!

Millwall has always been a club with a reputation – partially fair, partially not. Having begun life playing their football in the back garden of the Lord Nelson pub, the Lions moved in 1890 to a ground at East Ferry Road, opposite the Millwall docks, an area not known for the beauty of its surroundings. One player of the time was quoted as saying: 'I don't mind playing there, but I can't stand falling on the pitch. It takes weeks to get rid of the smell.'

Grounds for Complaint

Football today is a huge leisure industry, with many all-seater stadiums and state of the art facilities. But in the old days...well that's a different matter. How would you have fancied some of these goings-on?:

⊕ **At St. James' Park, Newcastle, players had to change in a local pub and butchers were allowed to graze their sheep on the pitch.**

⊕ **In their first game at Highbury, the Arsenal players washed in bowls of cold water after the match, and an injured player had to be wheeled away in a milk cart.**

⚽ In the early days of Grimsby Town's existence, players had to get changed in bathing huts brought up from the nearby beach to their Clee Park ground.

⚽ During World War II soldiers lived in the Main Stand at Exeter's St. James' Park ground. They carried out their training drills – presumably including shooting practice – on the pitch.

⚽ Montrose were so poor when they were formed that they had to borrow goal nets and hire out the pitch for animal grazing and as a circus venue just to make ends meet.

⚽ At Norwich's 'Nest' stadium there was a 50-foot high concrete wall which lined a cliff. At the top was a fence from which spectators could watch the game – talk about a bird's eye view.

☻ **When QPR played at a ground on Latymer Road in west London the players had to change in a nearby pub and run down the road to the pitch – but locals objected and took the club to court, saying that it 'lowered the tone' of the area.**

Recent discoveries have given more than an element of truth to fears that **Leyton Orient** could be well and truly dead and buried. English Heritage believed that there could be an ancient settlement – dating from 3,500 years BC – covering a half-mile area of Leyton which includes Orient's Brisbane Road ground. The possibility of a bronze age village emerging under the club's away south terrace meant that English Heritage called a three month halt to chairman Barry Hearn's plans to redevelop that area of the stadium. 'Perhaps they could unearth us a new striker,' joked Hearn at the time.

Scottish Third Division club **Dumbarton** have been at their present home longer than any other side in the world. Founder members of the Scottish League and at one time one of the country's top sides, The 'Sons' moved into their Boghead Park Stadium in 1879 – and have been there ever since. Only **Stoke** (at the Victoria Ground since 1878) had been in residence longer – but they moved to the all-new Britannia Stadium in the summer of 1997.

Tiny English club **Hartlepool** can make the strange boast of being the first football club to be bombed. German zeppelins dropped missiles on the club's Victoria Ground on 17th November 1916, and were later shot down. Strangely, the German government never responded to Hartlepool's demand for £2,500 compensation.

Talk about gruesome! When **Charlton Athletic** first moved to The Valley way back in 1919 the ground was a chalk pit with a well in it. Some of the earth used in the construction of the stadium came from a local hospital – and was full of old bones.

QUESTION

Hibernian have a state-of-the-art undersoil heating system in place at their Easter Road ground in Edinburgh, but in 1996 they still lost a game to the frozen surface. Why?

Scottish minnows **Queen's Park** are the world's only club to boast two home grounds. They play the majority of their games at the country's national stadium, Hampden Park in Mount Florida, Glasgow, but they also have another ground nearby, called New Lesser Hampden.

So we've seen how football came to be the world's greatest game, and we know about the players, managers and chairmen.

This can't be the new FIFA regulation ball

Answer: They forgot to leave the heating on overnight!

We've had the lowdown on the clubs, the grounds and the record-breakers. But what about the people who *really* matter ... the people who make football the awesome spectacle it is throughout the world. The fans ...

With Queen Victoria still on the English throne, the game of football is now firmly established and is casting its net right across Europe and the rest of the world for good measure.

In 1895 the Italian inventor Marconi presents the world with its first wireless and immediately plans for sports channels are set in motion across the globe. In less than 100 years, the broadcasting giants will go on to practically rule the world game.

In 1901, Victoria dies and is briefly succeeded by her son, Edward VII, a man who fully endorses playing away at every opportunity, particularly in the company of Jennie Churchill (Winston's mum) and the actress Lilly Langtry.

Meanwhile, in Peking, Chinese nationalists attack and lay siege to Europeans in the Boxer Revolution. Maybe they got upset because the Europeans had pinched their favourite old ball game.

1891 Goal nets introduced. This was to help referees decide whether the ball had gone between the posts or not ... of course, they still didn't ALWAYS get it right – they had to decide whether it crossed the line too. Penalty kick introduced, just to make the ref's job harder still.

1893 FA Cup Final moved to Crystal Palace.

PHENOMENAL PHACT!

In 1895 FA Cup holders Aston Villa decided to display the famous silver trophy in a Birmingham shop window — from where it promptly got stolen, melted down and was never seen again. No wonder their nickname is 'The Villans'. Fans from local rivals West Brom — who Villa had beaten in the Final 1-0 — weren't entirely sympathetic.

1904 FIFA is formed, with seven member countries. The British associations decide they don't need any 'bunch of foreigners' telling them how to run the game and refuse to join.

1906 Britain join FIFA.

QUESTION

Up until 1912, the goalkeeper was allowed to handle the ball anywhere in his own half. But that year, Portsmouth goalkeeper Matthew Reilly was behind one of the most controversial changes in the Laws of the game. Why?

Answer: Reilly was also an expert Gaelic football player back in his native Ireland and was well used to bouncing the ball as he dodged round opponents. His skill at racing up field in this manner — and then shooting from just inside his own half, prompted the FA to ban the handling of the ball outside the penalty area.

5 FANTASTIC FOOTBALL FANS

There is nothing in the world to match the sheer spectacle of a football crowd in full voice, with colour, humour and an electric atmosphere all part of what makes the big match such a wonderful occasion.

From the all orange Dutch supporters and their big bands, to the face-painted followers of countless clubs and countries across the globe, the supporters are all part and parcel of football at its best...

Now far be it from us to say that **Doncaster** fans are completely bonkers, but, well, all that boredom must have an effect, mustn't it? The Belle Vue club have never been out of English football's bottom two divisions and their lack of success has led 'Donny' fans to resort to making their own entertainment. At a home match in 1991 some fed-up fans started singing: 'Would you like a piece of cake?' to their bemused visitors. The police stepped in, but quickly gave up when they realised it was just a harmless chant. Mind you, what were they going to arrest them for … assault and battenberg? A week later Donny were away at Burnley, and as the game progressed they resorted to offering cake to the police and singing (to the tune of John Lennon's 'War is Over'): 'So this is Burnley, what have we done, we've lost here already, would you like a cream bun?'.

All clubs have their famous fans, Oasis' Gallagher brothers are famed for following **Manchester City**, for example, opera singer Placido Domingo is **Barcelona** bonkers and Absolutely Fabulous actress June Whitfield is a dyed-in-the-wool member of **Wimbledon's** Crazy Gang. But little **Wigan Athletic** can boast one of the most well-known of them all. Former Soviet President Mikhail Gorbachev – him with the bird-bob on his head – was assistant secretary for a Russian side called Metallist Khartrov who played a friendly against Wigan at Springfield Park back in 1969/70. Legend has it that the Russian politician was so taken with the little town and its pier that he has remained an Athletic supporter ever since. Wonder if he could get them a perestroikas?

And you can quote me on that …
'Can we play you every week?' Heard from Bolton fans after a 4-1 victory at Middlesbrough ended a long losing streak.

They know how to celebrate a good victory in South America. Fans in **Bolivia** were so excited when their national side beat Uruguay 3-1 that they lit fireworks in the street to celebrate. Unfortunately a stray rocket landed on a house and set fire to it, the fire spread out of control and by the end of the party some 40 homes were wrecked and 150 people left homeless. Still, it was a good win!

Tiny Scottish club **Stenhousemuir** have provided footballing inspiration for at least one Indian football fan. There is a branch of the Stenny fan club in Chenigarth, where clairvoyant Ravindra Soni lives. Ravi fell in love with the club during a spell living in Scotland and is still arranging sponsored trips from India to see the Warriors play. Thing is, if he's a clairvoyant, surely he knows the result before he leaves home.

Some supporters will go to almost any lengths to see their team. Spaniard Ramon Muzo cycled 1,100 miles from his home on Majorca to watch **Spain** take part in the World Cup finals in Italy in 1990. He arrived on the eve of their opening game, against Uruguay, and stayed for 13 days before he, and his country, departed the competition.

But Ramon was lucky compared to **Grimsby Town** fan Mike Rowell who, in 1996, decided to cycle to West Ham to watch his side in FA Cup Fourth Round action. Having completed the 180-mile trip from England's East Coast to London, Mike arrived at the Hammers' Upton Park ground to discover that the match had been called off due to a frozen pitch!

The day that **German** fan Frederick Baum lost his job proved to be the luckiest of his life! Frederick was clearing out his desk when he came across an old pools coupon, which he decided on a whim to fill in. He had never done the pools before and had no idea what the coupon was doing in his desk – but he still won £400,000.

Swiss supporters had to seek special permission in the 1994 World Cup to take their famous cow bells to America. With all the noise generated at soccer matches you wouldn't think that a few cow bells would create such a problem. Obviously the authorities wanted the Swiss to be seen but not HERD!

> **And you can quote me on that ...**
> *'Score in a minute, we're gonna score in a minute.'*
> **Crystal Palace supporters look on the bright side –
> 20 minutes after the end of a game they lost 9-0 against
> Liverpool at Anfield in September 1989.**

In England during the late 1980s a new fad came to the sport. Fed up with constant talk about hooligans and the many problems of following football in those dark days of away fan bans and membership cards, large numbers of fans began to show their support for a particular team by the carrying of inflatables at football matches. It probably all began at **Manchester City**, where blow-up bananas were all the rage, but among other clubs to grab the attention in those early days – before all and sundry caught on – were **Grimsby Town**, who lived up to their 'Mariners' nickname with hundreds of inflatable 'Harry the Haddocks' that greeted the players at every game. Elsewhere we saw balloons, glove puppets, bald 'wigs' and, rather bizarrely, **Chelsea** fans serenading their favourites with sticks of celery and a song far too rude to print in these pages. **Brentford** fans even organised a cheese cruise, where supporters were invited to take various different cheeses with them on a trip up the River Thames to Woolwich when the 'Bs' played Charlton in an FA Cup tie.

And talking of **Charlton**, the south London club can boast some of the most determined fans around. After the club were evicted from their traditional home at The Valley in 1985, and forced to share with distant neighbours Crystal Palace, and later West Ham, the 'Addicks' fans spent several years battling for a return to their happy hunting grounds. In 1990 they formed 'The Valley Party' and stood for office in a local election, polling a whopping 14,838 votes in 60 council seats. In 1992 those loyal and remarkable fans were granted their dearest wish – a return to The Valley.

They do things differently in **Ireland**, where soccer success is a relatively new phenomenon and fans and players tend to party together. After beating England 1-0 in Stuttgart in the 1988 European Championships the celebration went long into the night, with fans, players and staff linking up for the mother of all parties. Veteran defender Paul McGrath – fond of a celebratory beer himself – explained: 'We had to let the supporters in – none of us knew how to play the fiddle.'

BACK TO SQUARE ONE

'Back to square one' is a well-known saying that is often used by people in everyday life. It means to return to the beginning or to start again. But not a lot of people realise that the phrase has its origins in football. Back in 1927 – long before the days of colour TV and satellite dishes – listeners often found it difficult to understand what radio commentators were going on about. In order to make the game easier to follow a diagram of the pitch, split into numbered squares, was printed in the Radio Times. A commentator, such as the famous Derek McCulloch, would then call out the number of the square where the action was taking place. After a goal was scored, the ball would always return to square one, the centre of the pitch.

The **Scottish** national side are widely recognised as having some of the most loyal and good humoured fans around – and over the years they have needed to be, as great achievement has almost inevitably been followed by immense let-down. Tales abound of Scots selling all their possessions, divorcing their wives and travelling to far-flung corners of the globe only to see their heroes lose to the likes of Peru and Costa Rica. Apparently there are places in Spain still full of Scottish fans who travelled out to the 1982 World Cup and never went home. But as legendary Scotland manager Jock Stein said after that tournament: 'We do have the best fans in the world – but I've never seen a fan score a goal.'

The fans are football's unsung heroes – the people who keep the colour on the terraces, the passion in the play and – at many clubs – the money in the bank.

But what keeps us cheering, booing and coming back for more …

During World War I a very famous match takes place on Christmas Day 1916, when Allied and German soldiers throw down their guns and have a kickaround in 'no man's land' between the trenches. Once it is all over, and shirt-swapping and handshakes are completed, the soldiers return to their jobs – and start blowing merry hell out of each other once again.

But, with the end of the Great War, Europe and the world looks forward to lasting peace and, of course, the opportunity to continue playing football in more serene circumstances.

Sadly, Hitler's Germany soon decide on an unscheduled away fixture in Poland, followed quickly by 'visits' to most of the rest of Europe too. After six years of bitter fighting from Britain to Turkey and from America to Russia, the Germans are denied the opportunity to make themselves the world's most powerful team (off the pitch at any rate).

In 1947 India is granted independence from England, while two years later Eire declares itself the Republic of Ireland. At least one of these countries will soon be showing the Brits how to succeed on the football field.

DEBUT DAYS

Everyone respects Brazil as being one of the best footballing countries in the world. The nation that gave us such stars as Pele, Jairzinho, Zico, Romario and Ronaldo has lifted the World Cup on four occasions and draws huge crowds wherever their famous yellow, blue and white kit is on show. But the Brazilian legend grew from humble beginnings. Their very first game was back in 1914, when they assembled to play touring Exeter City, who were not even in the English Football League at the time.

1923 The FA Cup Final is staged at Wembley for the first time, in front of an estimated crowd of 200,000.

1928 Showing all the decision-making skills of a UN Peace envoy with a whistle, Britain leaves FIFA again.

1930 The first World Cup takes place, and is won by Uruguay. England decide that it's a terrible idea and will never catch on, so decide not to enter.

1946 Guess what? Yep, Britain rejoins FIFA.

1950 Tired of being so good and nobody else knowing it, England finally relent and enter the World Cup, where they are promptly beaten 1-0 by the United States in one of the all-time biggest shock results. Some British papers were so convinced that the scoreline was wrong that they listed it as 10-1 to England instead!

1951 The white ball first comes into official use. Before now matches had been contested with brown leather balls which needed to be laced up before games. When it rained these balls became incredibly heavy and could even knock a player out!

1953 Things go from bad to worse as England lose a match to overseas opposition at Wembley for the first time – and how. Hungary come to town and inflict a 6-3 thrashing on Walter Winterbottom's boys. A year later the Hungarians win the return match 7-1 in Budapest – still England's worst defeat. Forty years later, Graham Taylor resigned as England manager six days after his team had BEATEN San Marino 7-1 at Wembley in a World Cup Qualifier.

1955 Fed up with being in the dark all the time, some bright spark invents floodlights to make evening games more interesting. The first match under lights is Kidderminster Harriers against Brierly Hill Alliance in the FA Cup Qualifying Round.

1958 In a bid to beat the freezing weather, Everton become the first team to experiment with an electric heating system under the pitch. Thirty years later, Chelsea chairman Ken Bates tried to use electricity in a different way – he wanted to erect an electric fence to keep fans in their place.

6 FANTASTIC FOOTBALL FOUL PLAY

All over the world millions of punch-ups, bust-ups and downright dodgy dealings are going on even as you read this.

We all know about trouble on the terraces – but as controversial manager Brian Clough once said: 'Football hooligans? Well there's the 92 Club Chairmen for a start.'

Take a look at some of the fantastically foul goings-on within the game itself ...

DANGEROUS GAME FOOTBALL

Next time you're watching a South American side and somebody screams 'shoot!', you'd better take cover – they might mean it!

In 1994, Colombian World Cup star Andres Escobar, was shot dead after a bust-up in a car park but more importantly after scoring an own goal for the United States which effectively knocked Colombia out of the 1994 World Cup. The story was that Escobar's careless kick had ended up costing some South American drug barons millions of pounds in lost bets. And you thought that Gareth Southgate had it bad?

In 1983 a Colombian Justice Minister claimed that six of the country's top clubs were financed almost entirely by cash obtained from illegal drugs operations.

Another Colombian, Deportivo Independiente player Arley Antonio Rodriguez, was blasted by gunmen who were trying to steal his motorbike, a youth was also killed in the incident.

Or how about Mexican Carlos Zomba, who scored four times for Atlanta in a League match against Los Apaches. At the end of the game, hot-shot Zomba was shot four times himself, and never played again.

Meanwhile, Carlos Alberto Oliviera – head honcho of Brazil's FA – was doing a radio interview alongside Marcia Braga, the President of one of Brazil's biggest clubs, Flamengo, when the pair had, shall we say, a bit of a disagreement over a couple of things. Silvio Guimaraes, from the Pernambuco State FA, got so angry that he threw a chair at Braga, while Mr Oliviera went one better and threatened – on air – to go home, get his gun and finish off the argument 'once and for all'. Maybe that's what they mean by letting a shoot-out settle things.

Then there was the Brazilian Club Chairman who shot one of his own star performers dead after the player demanded a transfer following a disagreement over pay.

Of course, it's not just in South America that Club Chairmen get away with murder – figuratively speaking. Along with Sporting Lisbon, Portuguese giants Benfica were involved in one of the most fierce contract struggles of all time when they signed the legendary Eusebio in 1961. The gifted Eusebio was a player with Sporting's nursery club, Laurenco Marques, in Mozambique, but when he arrived in Portugal he was promptly met off the plane by representatives of the Benfica club and 'kidnapped'. Eusebio was forced to lie low in an Algarve fishing village until all the fuss had died down. It was all worth it as far as Benfica were concerned, as Eusebio went on to become one of the finest players of all time.

If you thought the latest game you played in was rough – then think again. Playground scraps or park brawls are nothing compared with what went on when Argentinian side Boca Juniors took on Peruvian club Sporting Cristal in South America's Copa Libertadores back in 1971. A huge punch-up took place after a bad tackle and resulted in 19 players being sent-off, with 16 of them later being sentenced to 30 days in jail. The three that 'got away with it' only did so because they were so badly injured they were rushed to hospital. Not surprisingly, the match was abandoned!

BEER WE GO, BEER WE GO ...

A special summer match in Germany produced an amazing result. A beer hall owner in Werdohl offered 11 bottles of beer for every goal his local team scored. Not to be outdone, a rival offered the same for his team. Werdohl won the match, but both sides celebrated long into the night – the final score was 24-23.

FANTASTICALLY FEARSOME FOOTBALLERS

On 14th December 1987, QPR defender **Mark Dennis** was sent-off for the 11th time in his professional career, including two dismissals for after-match offences in the player's tunnel. At that time he had also been cautioned 64 times in ten years and twice been charged with disrepute following newspaper articles. A skilful footballer with a good left foot, Dennis, unfortunately, fully deserved his nickname of 'Mad Mark'. However his record is nothing compared to that of ex-international **Willie Johnston**, who amassed a staggering 21 sendings-off during his career with Rangers, West Brom, Vancouver Whitecaps, Hearts and Scotland.

QUESTION

See which other hard-men can you match up with their nicknames...

Stuart Pearce	Chopper
Julian Dicks	Gentleman
Norman Hunter	Razor
Ron Harris	The Bash
John Fashanu	Bites Yer Legs
Neil Ruddock	Psycho
Jack Charlton	The Terminator

Yugoslavia's Macedonian Regional League came up with a couple of **odd results** at the climax of the 1978/79 season, and it's not too hard to see why the games aroused the suspicion of the authorities. The village sides of Ilinden and Debarce were running neck and neck for the title, with only goals scored separating them as they went into the final matches. On the day in question, Debarce won 88-0 at Gradinar, while Ilinden were scoring a mere 134 without reply at home to Mladost. It surprised nobody that all four teams were suspended!

A candid camera-style TV show fooled **AC Milan** manager Adriano Galliani into thinking that some of his side's top players had been kidnapped. Galliani was taken to a city centre flat, where he was shown video footage of Roberto Baggio, Gianluigi Lentini and Gianluca Sordo being held by terrorists. He was let in on the joke only after agreeing to the kidnappers' demands that he select himself for the first team.

TRUE OR FALSE?

In the 1983 African Cup-Winners' Cup Second Round a match between Stationery Stores and Asecs was abandoned after a series of punch-ups, started by enraged Stationery players for no apparent reason.

On the subject of black magic, in 1997 the Kenyan Football Federation officially 'banned' **witchcraft**, saying that its use had reached 'epidemic proportions'. Six international players were slapped on the transfer list by the

Answer: True. At the start of the second-half the Asecs goalkeeper was seen to bury something behind his goal - and the players were convinced that black magic was being put to work!

Kenya Ales team after it was revealed that the dirty half-dozen 'paid more attention to ju-ju [witchcraft] than their own coach'. Wonder if that's the 'little spark of magic' that managers so often talk about winning games.

Peruvian club side Melgar were the victims of a curse put on them by a former player in 1979. They were having a disastrous season before a member of the club's staff had the bright idea of soaking the players' shirts in a magic potion to chase away the evil spirits. It worked, as Melgar went on to win their crucial play-off games and thus avoid relegation.

The final word on this matter goes to South Africa. When mighty Qwa Qwa Stars travelled to play lowly Moroka Swallows the game was delayed for ten minutes so that the Stars' shirts could dry. They claimed that the Swallows had splashed 'magic water' on them before the game and refused to play until it had dried. The game ended in a 1-1 draw.

SHOOTING PRACTICE

Some time ago some Belgian players were training in thick fog just before Christmas. A passing hunter saw them and, believing them to be deer, opened fire with his shot-gun. Two of the players were hit by grape-shot and spent the next few days sitting on very soft cushions!

Legendary Liverpool manager Bill Shankly once famously commented: 'People say that football is a matter of life and death. It isn't. It's far more important than that.' While all football fans will recognise the sentiments of that statement, there are obviously more important things in the world than 22 people kicking a ball about.

In the Qualifying matches for the 1970 World Cup in Mexico, football literally became a matter of life and death for thousands of central Americans. Honduras and El Salvador had been at loggerheads for many years when the two nations were drawn to play each other in a three-match play-off to decide who would travel to Mexico '70. Honduras won the first match 1-0, while El Salvador struck back by taking the return 3-0, setting up a grandstand finale. El Salvador duly won the game 3-2 – but the result kicked off border skirmishes followed by an all-out war between the two nations which saw more than 2,000 people killed in the fighting and upwards of 100,000 made homeless.

Elsewhere, Cameroon club Canon had a classic Semi-Final victory over Nigeria's Bendel Insurance on their way to winning the African Champions Cup in 1980. There was a bad aftertaste, though, since the result caused riots in Benin, Nigeria, and eight people were killed.

PHENOMENALLY ROTTEN
REFEREES ...

As we all know, the referee is the boss, the king, the main man, and everything he says is correct. Or something. Whatever we think of him, the man with the whistle is all powerful – but sometimes he can be TOO powerful ...

⚽ A local League referee in Bogota, Colombia, was once suspended for 'showing a distinct measure of favouritism to the home side'. How did they know? Well, he did award them *seven* penalties in just one game.

⚽ English ref Kelvin Morton didn't go quite that far in 1989 – he awarded 'only' five spot-kicks in a 'derby' match between Crystal Palace and Brighton. Palace duly missed with three of their four attempts, while Brighton netted their solitary effort...but still lost the match 2-1.

⚽ Ivan Robertson made a little bit of history in 1968, when he became the first referee to score a goal in a senior game. Manning the whistle in a match between Barrow and Plymouth he accidentally deflected the ball into the Barrow net – scoring what proved to be the winner for Plymouth. Bet he was a popular man.

⚽ In Italy, the power of the referee once reached beyond the grave. Having been sent-off playing for his local club, Luigi Coluccio was handed a one-match ban – no problem with serving it, he was dead. Poor old Luigi had been gunned down outside a bar in southern Italy nine days before his punishment was decided by the Italian FA. It must have been a grave offence.

⚽ Egyptian referee Mr Kandil was obviously a brave man. Officiating at a 1970 World Cup match between hosts Mexico and qualifiers El Salvador, he blew for a foul to El Salvador – only for the Mexicans to quickly take the kick themselves and score. Amazingly, he allowed the goal to stand.

⚽ But perhaps the most dramatic refereeing decision ever made came in Tripoli, Libya, in July 1996. Al-Aadi, the son of national leader Colonel Gaddafi, was a supporter and patron of Al-Ahly, one of Tripoli's 'big two' clubs. In the Tripoli 'derby' that year, Al-Aadi was in his usual seat at the ground, surrounded as always by gun-toting 'minders', when his club scored a goal which should never have been allowed. Never mind his reputation, the ref was worried about keeping his head and shoulders together and awarded the goal. A bit of an upset, but no real problem, right? Wrong. There was a huge riot, gun-firing, 50 spectators injured, 20 either shot or crushed to death and the Libyan League was suspended.

Of course, the ref doesn't get everything his own way ...

⚽ In Argentinian TV coverage, every time a penalty is awarded a cartoon ref strides across the screen ... led by a guide dog!

⚽ And in Brazil a club president was so angry when a penalty was awarded against his team that he sprinted onto the pitch and shot the ball to pieces with his pistol. Rather sensibly the referee agreed that, yes, maybe it had all been a terrible mistake, and changed his mind, awarding an indirect free-kick instead.

⚽ Another ref who wisely altered his decision was the fellow in charge of the Bolivian encounter between Blooming and San Jose. With the scores finely balanced at 1-1, the ref awarded a controversial penalty to Blooming. A pitch invasion swiftly followed, with San Jose fans forcing the referee to get on his knees and beg forgiveness.

⚽ Have you ever heard of a referee being sent-off? Well it happened in Brazil, when Luiz Vila Nova was in charge of a League match. He sent off Semilde of Urubuetama, who promptly insulted the ref as he was leaving the pitch. Much to the player's astonishment, Vila Nova then threw down his notebook and landed a right-hook on Semilde's chin. Once Semilde recovered from the shock he tried to kick the referee, who then went on the attack again. Officials raced on and removed them both, with a linesman having to take over for the rest of the game.

⚽ Another incident which had the fans laughing occurred in Peru in 1974. During a League match in Chimbote, referee Alipio Montejo awarded a goal which linesman Gonzalo Morote had flagged offside. The linesman ran on to the pitch to discuss the decision, a heated argument took place and a punch-up swiftly ensued. For once it was a case of the players splitting up warring officials.

⚽ But spare a thought for Welsh ref William Ernest Williams, who was attacked and killed in his dressing-room after a match between Wattstown and Aberaman Athletic in 1912. His attacker was later jailed for manslaughter.

LONG KUWAIT FOR FOOTBALL

Football began in Kuwait towards the end of the last century, but it was not until the 1930s that the Kuwaitis themselves got involved. Until then they had been banned by their religion and local customs from having anything to do with the sport.

And you can quote me on that ...
'I shouldn't have been upset at losing to Benfica. After all, they have the best players, the best referees and the best linesmen.' Sore loser Jimmy Hagan, manager of Portuguese club Vitoria Setubal, in 1980.

QUESTION

Why did Portuguese referee Carlos Calheiros' dream holiday in Brazil land leading club Porto in hot water?

Answer: Because it was later discovered that Porto had accidentally paid the £3,000 cost of the trip.

QUESTION

When Barbados played Grenada in a cup tie the teams suddenly started acting strangely with five minutes left. What did they do?

A. Run around with their shirts pulled over their heads.

B. Start singing to the crowd.

C. Start shooting at their own goals.

And you can quote me on that ...
'If Ron Harris was in a good mood he'd put iodine on his studs before a game.' TV pundit Jimmy Greaves speaking about football's 'good old days'.

EARLY BATHS

It's not often that a player is sent-off without even setting foot onto the pitch – but that's exactly what happened to Anzola's Marcho Boschetti. Having warmed up, and about to enter the fray as a substitute, Boschetti was caught short and relieved himself behind the dug-out. Unfortunately for him he was spotted by the ref – who promptly red-carded him for ungentlemanly conduct. SOAP

Answer: C. Barbados had to win by two clear goals and were 2-1 up. However, if the game went to a penalty shoot-out whoever won would be credited with a 2-0 victory, exactly what Barbados needed. So as the minutes ticked away they started shooting at their own goal to credit Grenada with a goal and force the penalty shoot-out. Grenada realised what was going on and started shooting at their own goal as well, so that Barbados couldn't bend the rules!

Another Italian, Paolo Ammoniaci, lasted a little longer than Boschetti – he was on the pitch for a full 25 seconds before getting his marching orders! Brought on by Lazio as a tactical last minute substitute, Ammoniaci entered the fray as the opposing teams were arguing over a free-kick. He was almost immediately sent off after pretending to have been the player kicked!

But even that pales into insignificance alongside the record of Giuseppe Lorenzo, who was dismissed after just 10 seconds of a match between his club, Bologna, and Parma on 9th December 1990. Lorenzo was sent for his very early bath after striking an opponent.

In the World Cup, the quickest dismissal belongs to Uruguay's Jose Batista who lasted a mammoth 55 seconds before being sent off against Scotland in Mexico on 13th June 1986.

Coaches often talk about defensive players 'going to sleep', meaning a loss of concentration at a vital moment. But in Chile a team really did begin to nod off during a game. Wen Ceslao Aguilera, a member of the medical staff at Third Division Iberia, admitted giving his players sleeping pills before an important match against rivals FC Mulchen. He had taken a £200 bribe.

INSURANCE POLICY

In November 1997 Hungarian First Division club Haladas Szombathely lost the use of two of their players in unusual circumstances. Illness? Injury? Transfer? No. The pair had their registrations seized by the Vas County Social Security Fund, a state body which collects health and social security payments. The Fund insisted it would sell both players if Haladas failed to come up with 10 million forints (approx. £30,000) which they owed in national insurance payments.

Now we all know about Eric Cantona's karate-kick attack on Crystal Palace fan Matthew Simmonds during a match at Selhurst Park in 1995. Eric, who had a history of disciplinary problems, was fined and banned from the game for nine months. But what about the behaviour of South African defender Ahmed Gora Ebrahim, a star player with the country's Rabali Blackpool club? Ahmed was so incensed at being substituted during a game that he karate-kicked his coach, Walter Rautmann on his way off the pitch. The Austrian Rautmann was rushed to hospital with a kidney injury.

QUESTION

What is Botafogo player Guga's main claim to fame?

Of course, any player who breaks the rules in a big way can expect a fine, ban or both. But it's unlikely that any of today's players will match the punishment handed out to Trinidadian footballer Selwyn Baptista in the 1950's. Baptista was banned for 1,000 years after playing in a cup game … the day after he should have started a two-year suspension.

And you can quote me on that …
'Romeo Benetti – I was at a social function with him the other week and it was the first time I'd got within ten yards of him that he hadn't kicked me. Even then I kept looking over my shoulder.' Nervous ex-England international Kevin Keegan discusses the great Italian defender.

Answer: He came on as sub in a bad-tempered Brazilian local derby match against Flamengo, during which five players and a coach were sent-off, and nine others booked. Guga came on, scored the winner and was then sent-off – all in the space of ten minutes!

FANTASTIC FOOTBALL FLASHBACK

The 1960s prove to be a time of massive social change, with among other things, the death penalty and racism officially outlawed in Britain.

As the music of the likes of the Beatles and America's Elvis Presley begin to offer young people a different outlook on life and a new-found freedom of expression, so footballers begin to engineer their own departure from the rigid structures of before...

1961 Jimmy Hill is head of the Professional Footballers' Association (PFA) and gets the maximum wage removed. There is a sensation as England star Johnny Haynes is paid a whopping £100 a week! Most players wouldn't even get out of bed for that these days.

1965 Ten players, including England internationals Tony Kay and Peter Swan, go to prison after being found guilty of match-fixing. Substitutes are introduced for the first time, but are only allowed to replace injured players.

QUESTION

Keith Peacock, of Charlton, made an unwanted piece of history on 21st August 1965, what was it?

Average or Difference?

The FA's decision in 1975 to change the system for separating teams level on points from Goal Average to

Answer: Keith became the first player to be taken off under the new substitution rule.

Goal Difference brought a huge sigh of relief from schoolkids and football anoraks all over the country, whose brains had been overloaded trying to work out the old system. It worked like this:

Anytown United and Somewhere City finish level on points at the top of the League. Anytown have scored 80 goals and conceded 40, while Somewhere have scored 40 and let in 19.

Under goal average, boring, boring Somewhere would win the League, with a goal average of 2.11 against Anywhere's figure of exactly 2. This was worked out like this:

Goals Scored ÷ Goals Conceded = Goal Average

With goal difference, Anywhere would be rewarded for being miles more entertaining and finish top of the League. And quite right too. Goal difference is reached by:

Goals Scored − Goals Conceded = Goal Difference

Confused? Thought so. These days, the Football League separate teams in a much simpler way – if teams are level on points, whichever team scores most goals finishes higher.

1966 Having got round to deciding that maybe the World Cup isn't such a bad thing after all, England go and upset everybody by winning the flippin' thing. Geoff Hurst scores a hat-trick, some people thought it was all over, and it was then.

1975 The FA decide that goal difference is a much fairer way to separate teams that finish on the same points than the goal average system which has been in force since 1895. Nice quick decision then.

7 FANTASTIC FOOTBALL KITS

Never mind 4-4-2 or 3-5-2. Forget about sweepers, wing-backs or playing 'in the hole'. The most pressing concern for many clubs these days is what to wear! An appropriate colour and design is more important than ever.

This not only allows for the players to recognise each other, and for the fans to recognise their players, but it also provides the opportunity for a huge marketing and money-making operation.

Believe it or not, replica shirts, scarves and hats are a relatively new phenomenon, but the club's money-men are hard at work even as you read this, trying to think up new and ever more crafty ways of parting supporters from their hard-earned cash.

What should you go for? Red has been scientifically proven as the most 'successful' colour, but we can't all play in red. Where's the fun in that? Do you choose stripes, hoops, halves, quarters, chevrons, stipples or even some of the more strange 'bird bob' effects of recent years?

Even the fashion industry is getting in on the act, with catwalk-designer Bruce Oldfield called into to revamp Norwich City's home strip for the 1997/98 campaign. Meanwhile, a shirt recently worn by England goalkeeper David Seaman was memorably – and accurately – described as looking like 'an explosion in a paint factory'.

The style and make-up of football kit and equipment has changed dramatically since the early days of the beautiful game.

Back then, players generally wore golfing-style 'plus four' trousers, which were tucked into long socks which stretched up to the knee. A heavy woollen jersey which laced at the neck went on top and players usually sported a bobble hat or cap.

At the very beginning team-mates could distinguish each other only by the colour of a player's belt, hat or armband, but soon it became the custom for all members of the same side to wear similar coloured shirts – everything else could be as different as you wanted.

So how did we get from that, to today's multi-coloured disasters?

Kitsch Kit Corner!

Back in the 1870s a club called the Sheffield Zulus played all of their games dressed up in the garb of Zulu

warriors. It turned out to be a charity stunt – but can you imagine David Beckham and Co. dressed up like that these days?

1890 The custom begins of players wearing shin-pads inside, instead of outside, their socks. Before that it didn't matter what colour socks you wore – they couldn't be seen anyway!

Kitsch Kit Corner!

Talk about crazy kits – Blackburn Rovers once played an FA Cup Final in white evening suits! Having arrived in London to play Sheffield Wednesday in the 1890 Final, Rovers discovered there was a clash of colours,

and sent somebody out to the nearest gents outfitters to find a suitable alternative. Maybe they were making a statement, because Blackburn fans visiting London for the Final six years previously had been described by a magazine as: 'Northern barbarians...of uncouth garb and speech. A tribe of Arabs would not excite more amusement.'

Although in those days football was mainly a man's game, it was the women's teams of 1895 who first drew notice to the style and design of football kits. The *Manchester Guardian* of the day, reporting on a North v South women's match at Crouch End, revealed: 'The ladies of the 'North' team wore red blouses with white yolks and full black knickerbockers fastened below the knee, black stockings, red beretta caps, brown leather boots and leg pads.'

1900 The first recorded piece of product placement takes place on a football field, as racehorse owner Lord Rosebery persuades Scotland to take on England in his riding colours of primrose and white hoops. There's an old saying 'change your colours, change your luck' and Scotland respond by hammering the auld enemy 4-1 in Glasgow.

Kitsch Kit Corner!

Italian giants Juventus, a club founded by students, can thank an unlikely source for their world-famous black and white kit, which has made them one of the most distinctive clubs in Europe since the early 1900s. In 1903 the then infant Juventus (whose name translates as 'youth') returned from a trip to England having been donated a set of shirts by none other than ... Notts County. Before that, the Italians had played in a kit of all *pink*! Similarly, Spanish club Atletico Madrid owe their traditional red and white stripes to a visit from Sunderland.

1909   Goalkeepers begin to wear different coloured shirts to the rest of their team, so that referees know which players are actually allowed to handle the ball. The following year, kits become uniform, with players on the same side wearing similar coloured shorts and socks, as well as shirts. Goalkeepers can only wear shirts of royal green, royal blue, scarlet or white.

1921   Goalkeepers are now informed that they must wear yellow shirts for all internationals.

1924   The FA announce that it is obligatory for teams to have a 'change' strip different in colour to their 'home' kit. These must always be used when there is a colour-clash between the two sides.

1927   Arsenal 'keeper Dan Lewis blames his new shirt for Arsenal's defeat in the FA Cup Final (see *Fantastic Football Folk*).

1928   Arsenal and Chelsea experiment with wearing numbered shirts, but quickly abandon the idea as 'pointless'.

1933   Not put off by the earlier failure, the FA decide to use numbered shirts in the FA Cup Final. Everton's players wear 1-11, while Manchester City come out in 12-22.

1937   For the first time, England appear with numbers on their shirts. The players can't see why, they are famous enough as it is!

1939   Shirt numbering is officially introduced to football.

1955   Fashion trends in England begin to turn towards the new, shorter shorts worn by continental European and South American teams.

1970   The first steps of shirt sponsorship, as the England national team signs an exclusive kit deal with the 'Admiral' sportswear company. In a great display or 'one rule for one ...', clubs are forbidden to follow suit. Nowadays it is more unusual to see a club without shirt-front sponsors.

1972   Leeds boss Don Revie, never one to miss out on a new idea for publicity, makes his players wear numbered tags hanging from their sock tops. After each match the players toss the tags to the crowd as souvenirs.

1973 England midfielder Alan Ball regularly turns out in a pair of white boots.

Kitsch Kit Corner!

In a recent survey, football supporters voted Coventry's 1970's away strip of chocolate brown, with lighter brown stripes as the most unpleasant football kit of all time. Never mind Man Utd's players claiming they couldn't see each other in their grey away kit of the 1996/97 campaign, City's players didn't even want to see themselves in that hideous outfit!

1976 Malcolm Allison's Crystal Palace parade before games in designer tracksuits, each emblazoned with the relevant player's nickname.

1978 Shirtfront sponsorship is finally permitted, with Liverpool blazing a trail with a big money deal with Japanese electronics company 'Hitachi'. Clubs are not allowed to wear sponsored shirts when appearing on BBC TV though.

Kitsch Kit Corner!

In 1980 York City decided to jazz up their home strip by making the two stripes down the shirts meet to form a letter 'Y'. Everybody agreed that the new kits looked lovely – but York were upset when people started calling them the 'Y Fronts'.

Politics almost intervened in 1982, when Stockport County seriously considered changing their club colours. Why? Supporters felt that the traditional sky blue and white stripes too closely resembled the national strip of Argentina, with whom England was at war over the Falkland Islands.

1992 Referees get in on the act. With the formation of the new Premier League in England they move away from traditional all-black to a new green strip.

Kitsch Kit Corner!

Talk about a bunch of drips! Scottish club Clydebank were sponsored by pop group Wet Wet Wet in the early 1990s, while Oasis' Gallagher brothers are often linked with a shirtfront deal with their beloved Manchester City.

1993 Arsenal unveil an abstract yellow, blue and red away shirt which is described by respected TV commentator Brian Moore as being like 'something you'd reject for the kitchen curtains'. Despite its sartorial problems, the shirt goes on to become the Gunners' biggest-ever seller. There's no accounting for taste.

1994 Belgian international goalkeeper Michael Preud'Homme abandons his habit of wearing the shirt of Standard Liege – his first club – under his national jersey. The weather at the USA World Cup is just too hot.

1995 John Barnes and Stan Collymore, among others, regularly appear in red boots for Liverpool.

1996 Manchester United change out of their away strip of all grey for the second-half of a match against Southampton at The Dell. United later claim that their players 'couldn't see each other' in the shirts. It doesn't seem to help much, though, as Alex Ferguson's team wind-up 6-3 losers.

Kitsch Kit Corner!

Former Paris St. Germain goalkeeper Bernard Lama believes that wearing a pair of the opposition's socks during a game brings him luck. He gets

a friend to travel round the country buying him a pair before every match!

In Scotland, Celtic have always strongly resisted shirt numbering and numbered their shorts instead. It is only since the arrival of FIFA instructions forcing clubs to have shirt numbers that the Parkhead club have given in.

Once you've got your players all kitted-out you need to give them something to play for.

Every country has its own national competitions, but in Europe there are two main events which national sides look forward to more than anything else – the World Cup and the European Championship, and each have thrown up their share of strange goings-on …

FANTASTIC FOOTBALL FLASHBACK

Despite the social difficulties of the 1980s – particularly in Britain, where greed and self-interest creates many problems, not least in the shape of 'football hooligans' – the sport continues to grow and to enthral yet another generation of followers and players.

A very British sport has evolved into the world's most beautiful, and widely-played game.

1979   Trevor Francis becomes the first British player to be transferred for £1 million when he moves from Birmingham City to Nottingham Forest.

1987   The Football League introduce Play-Offs to determine relegation and promotion issues. This is a flash-back to the 1890s, when special 'test matches' were played for a similar purpose. It also spells an end for clubs in the lower leagues fighting to be allowed into the Football League, as automatic promotion and relegation is set-up between Division Four and the Vauxhall Conference.

1993   The FA decide to restructure the English Leagues and the FA Premiership is born. Division Two becomes Division One; Division Three, Division Two and Division Four, Division Three. There is no longer a Division Four. The biggest division now is between the rich clubs and the poor ones.

1994   In a bid to further increase global participation in the 'world game', the World Cup is played in the USA – the only major land-mass other than Australia where soccer popularity is limited. The tournament is a roaring success.

Every major tournament throws up its fair share of heroes and villians; its major moments of magic and some instantly forgettable foul-ups.

1996 Alan Shearer moves from Blackburn to Newcastle for a world record fee of £15 million.
1997 Manchester United win the Premiership for the fourth time in five seasons.

DOUBLE QUIZ

Manchester United completed an historic double 'Double' when they won the Premiership and FA Cup in the same season for the second time in 1995/96. They had previously managed the feat in 1993/94, but do you know which five other clubs have completed the 'Double', and in which seasons?

Answer: Preston (1888/89), Aston Villa (1896/97), Tottenham (1960/61), Arsenal (1970/71), Liverpool (1985/86).

8 FANTASTIC FOOTBALL COMPETITIONS

Here's a whistlestop tour of the big competitions of the past, and some of the true tales that emerged from each and every one …

WORLD CUP
1930 in URUGUAY

Winners: *Uruguay*
Runners-up: *Argentina*

Have you heard the story about the king who selected a World Cup squad? Well it happened in Romania after the country nearly failed to send a squad to Uruguay. In the end, young King Carol stepped in and instructed employers to give three months leave to any of their staff selected for the Romanian squad. He also issued pardons to any banned players who he wished to select. He didn't do too bad a job, either, as Romania thrashed Peru 3-1 before being knocked out by the hosts, and eventual winners, Uruguay.

1934 in ITALY

Winners: *Italy*
Runners-up: *Czechoslovakia*

The Czechoslovakian side which reached the Final in 1934 had no excuses for not knowing each other's style of play. The team was selected entirely from two clubs Sparta Prague and Slavia Prague. No other World Cup Finalist has had so few clubs represented in its line-up.

1938 in FRANCE

Winners: *Italy*
Runners-up: *Hungary*

After their amazing 6-5 defeat at the hands of Brazil in the 1938 World Cup, the beaten Polish team sent a telegram to their opponents congratulating them on their performance and wishing them luck for the remainder of the competition.

1950 in BRAZIL

Winners: *Uruguay*
Runners-up: *Brazil*

Widely regarded as the world's best team, Brazil are hard enough to beat at the best of times. So it was no surprise that Yugoslavia lost their crucial Group One match to the Brazilians in the 1950 World Cup – they started with only ten men. Star midfielder Rajko Mitic was about to sprint out onto the pitch when he knocked himself out on a wooden beam in the dressing room.

India withdrew from the tournament after FIFA decided that all players had to wear boots. The Indian players were used to playing barefoot and refused to change their ways at such a late stage.

1954 in SWITZERLAND

Winners: *West Germany*
Runners-up: *Hungary*

The tournament's top scorer was the legendary Hungarian Sandor Kocsis, who netted 11 goals as his country reached the Final. Kocsis was nicknamed 'The Man With The Golden Head' thanks to his brilliance in the air. He scored an awesome 75 goals in 68 games for Hungary.

1958 in SWEDEN

Winners: *Brazil*
Runners-up: *Sweden*

Little Northern Ireland qualified for the first time, and ended up with one of the stars of the tournament in the shape of five-goal Peter McParland. But it so nearly all went wrong for the Irish. Only a last minute change of heart from the Irish FA prevented a major let-down for the province. The Association had to overturn a Law forbidding their players to perform on a Sunday, after it transpired that several World Cup games had been scheduled for the 'holy day'.

1962 in CHILE

Winners: **Brazil**
Runners-up: **Czechoslovakia**

One of the most infamous and unpleasant games in World Cup history took place during the 1962 competition. Billed as the 'Battle of Santiago', hosts Chile literally fought out a 2-0 win over their rivals from Italy. Two Italians were sent-off, and a third left the field with a broken nose, while referee Ken Aston was given a police escort from the field. England's 0-0 draw with Bulgaria in the final Group Four game of the competition was dubbed 'the most boring match of the tournament' by watching journalists and broadcasters.

1966 in ENGLAND

Winners: **England**
Runners-up: **West Germany**

How times have changed. When Bobby Charlton scored a cracking second goal for England in the World Cup Semi-Final against Portugal, several of the Portuguese players shook his hand to congratulate him on the strike.

1970 in MEXICO

Winners: **Brazil**
Runners-up: **Italy**

Shortly before the 1970 tournament in Mexico, FIFA announced that any player designated to wear the No.13 shirt did not have to do so if he was superstitious.

1974 in WEST GERMANY

Winners: **West Germany**
Runners-up: **Holland**

England failed to reach the finals for the first time since they had begun entering the tournament in 1950. Needing a victory in their final qualifying match against Poland, England could only manage a draw. The man who denied them a place in Germany was Polish goalkeeper Jan Tomaszewski, who was outstanding between the sticks. Before the match he had been labelled a 'clown' by the controversial Brian Clough, who was commentating on the game, but it was 'Jan the Man' who had the last laugh as the wheels fell off England's World Cup challenge.

1978 in ARGENTINA

Winners: **Argentina**
Runners-up: **Holland**

Holland star Dick Nanninga earned himself the nickname of the 'laughing Dutchman' after he was sent-off against West Germany for laughing at one of referee Ramon Ruiz's decisions. Nanninga had only been on the pitch eight minutes at the time of his dismissal, but he recovered from this early set-back to play for his country in the Final.

1982 in SPAIN

Winners: **Italy**
Runners-up: **West Germany**

When people said that the players of Liberia were performing as if their lives depended on it, they were closer to the truth than they might have thought. It was reported that the ruler of the African country was so incensed with his team not performing well enough that he allegedly handed them a chilling ultimatum – play better or you'll be executed.

1986 in MEXICO

Winners: *Argentina*
Runners-up: *West Germany*

One of the most controversial goals of all time was scored during the 1986 tournament, as the brilliant Diego Maradona once again showed the dark side of his personality. With the score of Argentina vs England in the Quarter-Final deadlocked at 0-0 in the second-half, Maradona challenged England 'keeper Peter Shilton to a cross and clearly punched the ball into the net. The England players protested strongly, but the goal was allowed to stand and Argentina went on to win the World Cup. Asked about the 'goal' after the game, Maradona insisted that the 'Hand of God' had intervened. Mind you, Maradona's second goal in that game was so brilliant it could have come from the 'feet of God'.

1990 in ITALY

Winners: *Germany*
Runners-up: *Argentina*

Cameroon did remarkably well at the 1990 World Cup, becoming the first African entrants to get beyond the Group stage. They went all the way to the Quarter-Finals before being knocked out by England thanks to two penalties from Gary Lineker in the last ten minutes of the game. Their progress was all the more remarkable when you consider that their coach, Valeri Nepomniaschi, never spoke a word to his players. Nepomniaschi was Russian and had to use a translator to get his message across.

1994 in USA

Winners: *Brazil*
Runners-up: *Italy*

The Americans are generally recognised as world leaders in the 'hype' of everything from burger bars to cartoon characters to sports events. But the USA marketing machine wasn't operating too well at the opening ceremony for USA '94. Pop legend Diana Ross was meant to signal the climax of the event by blasting the ball into an empty net – but she missed, from two yards out! As if that wasn't bad enough, chat show host Oprah Winfrey then fell flat on her face walking off stage, with the eyes of the world upon her.

EUROPEAN CHAMPIONSHIP

1960 in FRANCE

Winners: *Soviet Union*
Runners-up: *Yugoslavia*

Sport is often seen as a perfect way to settle old scores, and to lift a nation's morale. But in 1960, the Spanish government felt that a major political point had to be made – and they made it. Spain withdrew its side from a Quarter-Final tie with the Soviet Union in the European Championship. The withdrawal was in protest at the Soviets' role in the Spanish Civil War.

1964 in SPAIN

Winners: *Spain*
Runners-up: *Soviet Union*

Four years later the Spanish had no such qualms, winning their first, and to date only, major trophy thanks to a 2-1 win over ... the Soviet Union. However, politics still played a part in the tournament as Greece refused to play their qualifying tie in Albania, citing fears for their players' safety. The two countries had technically been at war for more than 40 years!

1968 in ITALY

Winners: *Italy*
Runners-up: *Yugoslavia*

Midfielder Alan Mullery made sure of his place in history by becoming the first man ever to be sent off while playing a Full international for England. Mullery was dismissed on 5th June 1968 in a match against eventual Finalists Yugoslavia. Only three other players have taken an early bath while on senior England duty, they are: Alan Ball (vs Poland,

06.06.73), Trevor Cherry (vs Argentina, 15.06.77) and Ray Wilkins (vs Morocco, 06.06.86). There's obviously something about the month of June which goes to an Englishman's head!

1972 in BELGIUM

Winners: **West Germany**
Runners-up: **Soviet Union**

Even an illegal betting and bribes scandal couldn't deny West Germany their first victory in the European Championship. The Germans, who were denied several of their best players for the Quarter-Final against England, marched on to leave the Soviet Union as runners-up once again.

1976 in YUGOSLAVIA

Winners: **Czechoslovakia**
Runners-up: **West Germany**

Playing in his first ever international match, West Germany's Dieter Muller equalised for his country against Yugoslavia in the Semi-Final. Within ten minutes the newcomer had recorded a hat-trick!

1980 in ITALY

Winners: **West Germany**
Runners-up: **Belgium**

England goalkeeper Ray Clemence could probably be forgiven for conceding a goal in the 1-1 draw against Belgium in Brussels – the Liverpool number one couldn't see! Clemence received extensive treatment for eye problems after Belgian police used tear gas to break up fighting on the terraces in what was a dark day for English football.

1984 in FRANCE

Winners: France
Runners-up: Spain

So desperate were Czechoslovakia to win their qualifying game against Romania that for the last ten minutes of the match they had all eleven of their players camped around the Romanian penalty-box trying to score. The goal never came, and the Czechs failed to qualify for a tournament they had won eight years previously.

1988 in GERMANY

Winners: Holland
Runners-up: Soviet Union

Scottish defender Gary Mackay received a sackful of Christmas cards through the post from Ireland in 1988. Why? Well, Mackay scored on his international debut to give Scotland a 1-0 win over Bulgaria – leaving the Irish on top of their qualifying group and on their way to Germany 1988.

1992 in SWEDEN

Winners: Denmark
Runners-up: Germany

Denmark had trouble getting a team together for the 1992 finals in Sweden, which isn't too surprising as two weeks before the tournament they didn't know they were going to be there. Yugoslavia had qualified in their place, but the civil war in that country prompted UEFA to prevent the Yugoslavs from sending a team to Scandinavia. Many of the Danish players had to be recalled from holidays around the world, while manager Richard Moller-Nielsen wasn't too upset to cancel plans to redecorate his kitchen! The lack of preparation didn't do them much harm, though, as the great Danes went on to win the tournament!

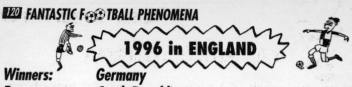

1996 in ENGLAND

Winners: *Germany*
Runners-up: *Czech Republic*

The Italians are famed as a nation who love style, culture and class – both on the pitch and off it. So when the Italian players discovered that there weren't enough hairdryers and mirrors at the dressing-room facilities of their training ground at Crewe and Alsager College they were understandably horrified. The squad promptly got together and coughed up half of the £20,000 needed to upgrade the facilities. Mind you, it was hardly worth their while, as the Azzuri found themselves on the way home before the Quarter-Final stage.

Award for the most bizarre goal celebration at Euro 96 went to Portugal, whose players raced over to the touchline to kiss a miniature replica flag every time they scored. The flag had been sent to the team coach Antonio Oliviera as a good luck charm from a young supporter, and every time his team found the net, Antonio would produce the flag for their urgent attention!

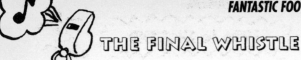

THE FINAL WHISTLE

And so, more than 500 years after organised football was banned under Edward II, the game has come to establish itself as the major sport in the world, with tournaments on every continent and millions of players in every corner of the globe. A very British sport has evolved into the world's most beautiful game. Now THAT'S fantastic!